P9-CAL-318

HOMETOWN HEARTS

The Soldier's Baby Bargain

BETH KERY

♦ **HARLEQUIN®** HOMETOWN HEARTS

Recycling programs
for this product may
not exist in your area.

ISBN-13: 978-0-373-21499-0

The Soldier's Baby Bargain

Copyright © 2012 by Beth Kery

Printed in U.S.A.

HOMETOWN HEARTS

SHIPMENT 1

Stranger in Town by Brenda Novak
Baby's First Homecoming by Cathy McDavid
Her Surprise Hero by Abby Gaines
A Mother's Homecoming by Tanya Michaels
A Firefighter in the Family by Trish Milburn
Tempted by a Texan by Mindy Neff

SHIPMENT 2

It Takes a Family by Victoria Pade
The Sheriff of Heartbreak County by Kathleen Creighton
A Hometown Boy by Janice Kay Johnson
The Renegade Cowboy Returns by Tina Leonard
Unexpected Bride by Lisa Childs
Accidental Hero by Loralee Lillibridge

SHIPMENT 3

An Unlikely Mommy by Tanya Michaels
Single Dad Sheriff by Lisa Childs
In Protective Custody by Beth Cornelison
Cowboy to the Rescue by Trish Milburn
The Ranch She Left Behind by Kathleen O'Brien
Most Wanted Woman by Maggie Price
A Weaver Wedding by Allison Leigh

SHIPMENT 4

A Better Man by Emilie Rose
Daddy Protector by Jacqueline Diamond
The Road to Bayou Bridge by Liz Talley
Fully Engaged by Catherine Mann
The Cowboy's Secret Son by Trish Milburn
A Husband's Watch by Karen Templeton

SHIPMENT 5

His Best Friend's Baby by Molly O'Keefe
Caleb's Bride by Wendy Warren
Her Sister's Secret Life by Pamela Toth
Lori's Little Secret by Christine Rimmer
High-Stakes Bride by Fiona Brand
Hometown Honey by Kara Lennox

SHIPMENT 6

Reining in the Rancher by Karen Templeton
A Man to Rely On by Cindi Myers
Your Ranch or Mine? by Cindy Kirk
Mother in Training by Marie Ferrarella
A Baby for the Bachelor by Victoria Pade
The One She Left Behind by Kristi Gold
Her Son's Hero by Vicki Essex

SHIPMENT 7

Once and Again by Brenda Harlen
Her Sister's Fiancé by Teresa Hill
Family at Stake by Molly O'Keefe
Adding Up to Marriage by Karen Templeton
Bachelor Dad by Roxann Delaney
It's That Time of Year by Christine Wenger

SHIPMENT 8

The Rancher's Christmas Princess by Christine Rimmer
Their Baby Miracle by Lilian Darcy
Mad About Max by Penny McCusker
No Ordinary Joe by Michelle Celmer
The Soldier's Baby Bargain by Beth Kery
The Maverick's Christmas Baby by Victoria Pade

Beth Kery holds a doctorate in the behavioral sciences and enjoys incorporating what she's learned about human nature into her stories. She writes in multiple genres, always with the overarching theme of passionate, emotional romance. Visit Beth at her website, www.bethkery.com.

My thanks to my editor, Susan Litman, for guiding me through this series with a sure hand and to Laura Bradford, my agent. As always, huge appreciation and a big hug to my husband for surviving yet another book with typical grace and patience.

Chapter One

Ryan Itani set down the magazine that he hadn't really been reading and glanced around the waiting room of the veterinarian's office. He wondered for the hundredth time if he shouldn't have tried to call Faith Holmes before surprising her while she was at work. If he were honest with himself, he'd have to admit he was worried that if he had called, she would have made an excuse not to see him.

Not that he blamed her. After what had happened last Christmas Eve, he technically couldn't hold it against Faith if she avoided him like the plague for the rest of her life. It would have been one thing if he'd stuck to his original mission that night three months ago—drive the twenty miles from Harbor Town to Faith's country house and pay his respects to his friend Jesse's widow. He'd been on three tours of duty with Jesse, both of them having served as pilots in the Air Force 28th Fighter Wing. He'd always respected Jesse's wife, Faith, always liked her openness and kind heart, appreciated her funny, warm letters to Jesse while they'd both been stationed in Afghanistan.

If he'd also thought Faith was one of the most stunning women he'd ever met, and that Jesse didn't deserve her, given his tendency for womanizing and infidelity, Ryan had kept that to himself.

Or at least he had until Christmas Eve.

Behind a partition, a dog barked loudly and a woman let out a shriek of alarm, bringing Ryan's straying thoughts back to the present moment. Another dog joined in the fracas. He heard a calm but authoritative woman's voice and went still. Faith had somehow passed him in the partitioned-off area of the waiting room where he sat. There must be another door leading from the exam rooms to the waiting area.

"Please put Knuckles's leash in the shortest, locked position, Mrs. Biddle." Faith's voice floated above the two dogs' loud barking. "You really shouldn't bring Sheba into the office without her container, Mr. Tanner. You can't blame Ivy and Knuckles for getting excited, seeing a cat unprotected like that. Jane, can you show Mr. Tanner and Sheba back to the examination room right away?"

"Sheba hates that container," a man grumbled. "*Sheba*, come back—"

"Wait, Knuckles! Oh, dear!" a woman moaned.

Ryan heard a sound like *omff* and sprung up from his chair. Rushing around the partition wall, he saw a gray, short-haired cat zooming across the room toward him. He bent and scooped it up into his arms without thinking before it had a chance to tear behind the receptionist's desk. When he straightened, he saw Faith in profile wearing a white lab coat, a skirt and pumps, her long, curling, dark hair rippling around her shoulders as she tried to restrain a scrambling Dalmatian puppy.

"Oh, no, Faith!" a short, blond-haired woman cried as she raced around the receptionist's desk. "Put him down. You shouldn't be holding a big dog like that in your condition."

"It's okay, I'm fine," Faith managed to get out as she soothed the squirming puppy.

"Here, I have the leash. Stupid of me, I somehow disconnected him when I was trying to restrain him by the collar," a frazzled-sounding, gray-haired woman in her fifties said as she grabbed Knuckles's collar. She reaffixed the leash, and Faith bent to deposit Knuckles on the floor.

Someone tapped on his forearm and Ryan pulled his glued gaze off the vision of Faith. What had the receptionist meant when she'd said *in your condition*? Was Faith ill? he wondered anxiously. He handed Sheba-the-cat to a husky black man in his twenties, nodding once distractedly when the man offered his thanks.

Faith was giving the gray-haired woman a weary smile. "Just remember—shortest, locked position for the leash for future office visits, Mrs. Biddle." She touched her belly as if to reassure herself.

It was a timeless gesture, and one Ryan immediately recognized.

Lightning-quick reflexes were an absolute must for a fighter pilot, and Ryan was known for being one of the fastest responders. In that moment, however, he uncharacteristically froze. An iron hand seemed to have clutched at his lungs, making breathing impossible. A thousand images and memories swept past his awareness as if he were a drowning man. One seemed to linger on the screen of his mind's eye: Faith answering the front door on Christmas Eve, her long, curling hair spilling around the snowy white robe she wore, her smile radiant, her large green eyes shining with emotion.

Ryan, I'm so happy you came.

Jesse would have wanted me to look in on you, make sure you were safe and sound.

He'd done more than just make sure Jesse's widow was safe and sound, though. A hell of a lot more.

Faith looked around and saw him standing in the waiting room. The stretched seconds collapsed.

"Ryan," she exclaimed in a shocked tone. The receptionist and all the patrons in the

waiting room turned to gape at him. "What are you doing here?"

"I flew in for business," he said shortly, referring to the new charter airline business he'd begun after leaving the Air Force last December. His gaze flickered downward over Faith's belly before he met her stare again. He'd forgotten how vividly green her eyes were.

"I think we'd better talk," he said.

She bit at her lower lip anxiously and took a step toward him. All the color had left her cheeks.

"Yes. I think we'd better."

Faith took off her lab coat and hung it on the hook behind the door of her private office. She cast a nervous glance at herself in the mirror mounted on the wall.

She couldn't believe Ryan was *here*. And he knew. Somehow he'd guessed about the baby. She'd seen the stunned realization in his dark eyes as they'd stood there in the waiting room.

She tried to smooth her waving, curling tresses—hopeless cause. She sufficed by pulling the mass up onto her head and clipping it in place. It was probably better to look a little more…*professional* for this meeting anyway, she told herself as she pulled a few coiling strands down to frame her face.

Ridiculous, the idea of being professional. Her relationship with Ryan might be described as "nearly nonexistent" or perhaps as "friendly acquaintances" or perhaps *"odd"* but hardly "professional." Not after Christmas Eve. Seeing him standing there, so tall, so commanding, so intense—it'd brought it all back. How he must be regretting that impulsive, inexplicable moment of blazing lust now.

Afterward he'd suggested they'd acted out of the emotional turmoil of their shared remembrance of Jesse's death in a chopper accident a year before. He'd also worried that their impulsive tryst had ruined the chances of him being there for her. As a friend.

A dull ache flared in her breast at the memory. It'd hurt, having Ryan say those things. Maybe it was true, that the incredible heat between them had been generated from an emotional backfire. She couldn't be sure what had happened on that night.

True, he'd been grieving the loss of he husband, in more than the obvious sen

She'd learned in a particularly painful way just months before his death that Jesse had been unfaithful. Yes, she'd been grieving his death, but not in the same way a woman would be if she'd been in a happy, trusting marriage.

Another thought had haunted her after she and Ryan had started to come back to their senses that night. Perhaps *Ryan* was like a lot of top guns, craving the next female conquest in the same way he might hunger for the jolt of adrenaline that comes from a faster jet?

Maybe Ryan was like Jesse.

She straightened her spine. None of that mattered now, she thought as she touched her stomach. She had more important things to consider—like the future of her unborn child.

Anxious but determined, Faith walked into the waiting room. The first thing she saw upon opening the door was Ryan. He sat facing her, his expression alert and stony. She met his gaze with effort.

His dark brown hair was short, but not military-short. It had started to grow out a bit since he'd become a civilian several months ago. His bangs fell onto his forehead, escaping the combed-back style. His lean jaw was dusted with whiskers. Although he looked entirely sober as he examined her, the lines that framed a firm, well-shaped mouth reminded her he was a man who liked to laugh.

When he wasn't still recovering from the shock of a lifetime, that is.

"Hi," Faith said shakily. She sensed an observant gaze and glanced behind the reception desk. Jane ducked her head and pretended to be utterly absorbed in the process of stuffing envelopes.

"We were able to clear about an hour and a half in my schedule, but I'm afraid we couldn't reach all of my patients' owners. I'm going to have to come back to work after we talk," she said nervously.

Ryan stood abruptly and came toward her. Funny—she'd only just left him in the waiting room forty-five minutes ago, but his height, his strength, his presence struck her anew. She found herself searching his features, trying to find some indication of what he was thinking or feeling. But Ryan wasn't known for being ice under pressure while performing complicated, dangerous flight maneuvers for nothing. Magnetically attractive and elementally male he might be, but she was learning he could be very difficult to read.

"Are you all right?" he asked tensely.

She blinked at the sound of his quiet, restrained tone. Perhaps he wasn't as impassive as she'd assumed.

"I'm fine. I'll explain everything." She waved toward the front door. She felt awkward and anxious. How did one go about telling a man that he was about to be a father? Not that the words really mattered. It was pretty clear to Faith that Ryan already guessed the result of that impulsive, foolish... *unforgettable* night.

"If we can just go somewhere private," Faith said.

He nodded once and touched her shoulder, encouraging her to go before him. Faith led him out the door. In a matter of days Holland, Michigan, would be blazing with color from its famous tulips and orchards, not to mention the brilliant sunsets over scenic Lake Michigan and Lake Macatawa. This afternoon, however, was a watered-down promise of what was to come. Weak sunlight fell on the budding trees and sprouting daffodils edging Faith's office building. She still felt the chill of winter in the mild breeze that touched her cheek.

"We can take my car," Ryan said, nodding toward a dark blue sedan in the nearly empty parking lot of her practice.

Faith's throat was too constricted with anxiety to respond. She said nothing as he opened the passenger-side door for her, although the very air between them seemed charged and electric with tension. They remained quiet as Ryan drove for a few minutes down the rural highway, and then pulled down a gravel lane that Faith knew led to a scenic lookout at Holland State Park. A moment later he stopped the car.

Both of them stared at the pale blue, rippling expanse of Lake Michigan and in the distance, the towering sand dune of Mount Pisgah. Faith struggled to find the right words, but nothing came. Nothing.

"You're pregnant," he said succinctly, breaking the silence.

"Yes."

A muscle jumped in his cheek and his hands tightened around the wheel. "Were you planning on telling me?"

"Of course," Faith said emphatically. She

blinked back the tears that suddenly burned in her eyes and met his stare. "I was planning on calling you and telling you next week."

He closed his eyes. "So it *is* mine," he said in a choked voice.

"Yes," Faith whispered. "There isn't…there hasn't been anyone else."

"You told me on Christmas Eve that you were on the pill."

She swallowed convulsively. Here it was—her lie exposed.

"Ryan, I didn't want you to worry. I knew that if I told you we had unprotected sex that night—"

"That I wouldn't leave," he said abruptly. "And that was what you wanted the most, wasn't it, Faith? For me to vanish from your life?"

She closed her eyelids and a few tears spilled down her cheeks. "It was a mistake. All of it. You know that as well as I do."

His hands closed around the steering wheel in what looked like a death grip. "I don't know what the hell I thought it was," he said tensely. "I still hadn't gotten my bearings straight when you told me you didn't think we should see each other anymore."

"You told me you thought it'd been a sort of…emotional backfire, that we'd acted so impulsively because of Jesse's death. You were Jesse's good friend, a comrade in arms. I was—"

"His wife," he said.

"His widow," Faith corrected. *If he'd lived, I would have been his divorced wife by Christmas,* she added in her thoughts. Misery, anger and guilt swept through her—a potent, poison mixture of emotions with which she'd become all too familiar.

She wasn't sure how much Ryan knew about Jesse's affairs. Did they talk about them, perhaps share stories of sexual conquests, compare notes? Had Jesse confessed to him about his affair with Captain Melanie Shane? Melanie was a member of their wing, after all. She'd been the pilot and only survivor of the helicopter crash that had killed Jesse. Ryan might know that Melanie had contacted Faith and revealed her affair with Jesse months before the accident. He might already know Faith had filed for divorce at the time of Jesse's death.

Then again, he might not.

Most importantly, if Ryan had known

about Jesse's infidelities, how much did that figure into what had happened between them at Christmas?

"When I said that thing about what happened between us being an emotional backfire, I was grabbing at straws," Ryan said in a low, vibrating voice. "I was looking for anything to help me understand how I could have taken advantage of a vulnerable woman—someone I care about. I returned to Michigan on Christmas Eve to offer support to my friend's widow. You know I always liked you…respected you, even if we'd only met a couple of times. What happened between us was the last thing I'd expected. I meant to make you feel better, but instead, I caused you harm," he said, wincing.

Her backbone stiffened. "You haven't *harmed* me. I'm thrilled about the baby, Ryan." He glanced at her, quick and wary, and she caught a glimpse beneath his stony, top-gun facade. For a brief second she saw the stark anxiety in his gaze. Her temporary irritation faded. She'd had three months to come to terms with the fact that her life was about to change forever. Ryan had had only an hour to absorb that mind-blowing reality.

"I don't expect you to be thrilled about it—at least not right off the bat," she said quietly. "It's a shock. I know it's the last thing on earth you thought would happen."

Her hushed voice seemed to reverberate in the air between them.

"I want you to know I plan on sharing custody with you. I hope we can work together to make things as secure and comfortable for the baby as we can," she said, breaking the taut silence.

His face looked rigid as he turned and stared out at the great lake. Faith took the opportunity of his averted gaze to drink in her fill of the image of him. He had a great profile—a strong chin, straight, masculine nose; firm, well-shaped lips. *Hard.* That was the impression one got when they looked at Ryan. Tough as steel, honed, fast nerves, a brilliant mind. His body had been hard and honed as well, but also warm, sensitive, delightful for a woman to mold against…touch.

She inhaled sharply, willing her straying brain to come to order. His aftershave tickled her nose, the subtle, spicy, clean male scent triggering a wave of sensual memories. She knew from *that* night that the scent clung especially rich there at his nape at the edge of his hairline.

Her cheeks grew warm.

"I can't believe we're having this conversation," he said after a pause, forcing Faith to focus. "I can't believe you're going to have a baby."

"*We* are," she said softly. He turned his head and met her stare.

"Are you really happy about it?" he asked.

"I'll admit that at first I was pretty bowled over. It didn't take me long to get used to the idea...become excited," she said quietly, her fingers brushing against her abdomen instinctively. She paused when she noticed Ryan's stare on her hand. A warm, heavy feeling expanded in her belly and lowered. Her fingers seemed to burn beneath his gaze. How was it that he so effortlessly had this effect on her? She saw his strong throat convulse as he swallowed.

"So...you're about three months along?" he asked gruffly.

"I just started my second trimester."

"And the doctor says—"

"The baby is perfectly healthy. I've already had an ultrasound," she said, wonder filtering into her tone. Some of the miracle of that

day came back to her unexpectedly. He was the father, after all, the cocreator of that tiny miracle she'd seen on the screen.

His expression looked flat. Faith realized she was witnessing a highly unlikely event first-hand—Major Ryan Itani in a state of shock.

"Ryan, are you all right?"

"Of course," he said. He blinked as if to clear the haze from his vision. "And you? You're healthy, as well?" he asked in a voice that struck her as strained.

She smiled reassuringly. "I'm fine. Completely healthy."

"What…what do you plan to do?" he asked after a moment.

"Do?" she asked bemusedly. "Well, have the baby, of course. Take care of it. Love it."

"All on your own?"

"I don't see why not. I have a good job. My practice is doing very well. I'm just as capable as any adult of taking care of a baby."

"Your parents moved to Florida a year ago," he said. "You don't have any other family remaining in the area, do you?"

"No, but that doesn't mean much. I doubt my parents would have been super excited to get involved anyway. They're pretty involved with their own life. But I have good friends in town, like Jane."

"Your office manager?" he asked doubtfully.

She gave him a surprised glance. "Did you meet Jane while I was seeing patients?" she asked, referring to earlier, when he'd waited for her at her office.

He nodded distractedly. "She introduced herself. Besides, you talked about her on Christmas Eve, remember? You'd spent that evening with Jane's family."

"Oh, right."

An awkward silence settled. It struck her how bizarre this situation really was. She'd only met Ryan in person on two other occasions before Christmas Eve—at summer picnics for families of members of the 28th Wing while Jesse and Ryan had both been based in the Bay Area. She'd liked Ryan very much, and knew that Jesse's admiration for him bordered on worship. Ryan and she were both from Michigan, and Ryan had regularly spent his summers in nearby Harbor Town, so they'd had that in common. She'd enjoyed talking to him. She may have been married at the time, but she wasn't blind. Ryan was a very attractive man. Still, he'd never been in the forefront of her mind. Aside from those casual social events and constantly hearing his name mentioned by Jesse, Faith had known little else about him.

Christmas Eve had brought knowledge, of course, of the lightning strike of passion variety. But sharing a wild moment of lust with a man hardly qualified as true intimacy.

Now they were going to have a baby together. The strangeness of the whole thing was almost mind-numbing.

"You don't have enough people around you for support, Faith. I'm sure Jane is a good friend, but it's not the same as a family. We even talked about that very thing at Christmas."

Her mouth fell open. He'd been so approachable one second, but now his serious tone sent a prickle of alarm through her. Surely he wasn't going to start dictating terms to her, was he? "I'll make do, Ryan. I'll figure things out."

"I'm all the way out on the West Coast."

"Well, I'm not moving."

He blinked, and she realized how emphatic she'd sounded. "Sorry—I know you weren't suggesting that, but well…please don't. Suggest it, I mean." She met his stare, hoping he'd understand. "I like my life here. I grew up in this area and think it'd be an ideal place to raise a child. I missed it during the years I traveled around with Jesse. Plus, I love my job. I'm proud of the practice I've built."

He studied his hands on the steering wheel. "You *should* be proud of it. You did it all on your own. Starting up this airline charter business, I know how much work that takes. How much dedication."

"Thank you for saying that," she said sincerely, some of her former tension draining out of her. "I don't blame Jesse for his job, or for the fact that it required him to be out of the country for a large chunk of our marriage. It forced me to be independent. I built my practice from nothing into something that's not only a thriving business, but an emotionally fulfilling one for me."

He studied her through a narrow-eyed gaze that she couldn't quite interpret. She avoided his laserlike stare, looking at her hands folded in her lap.

"I probably should get back to work," she said.

His hands slid along the steering will and he shifted the car into Reverse. He did a neat two-point turn and soon they were once again traversing the gravel drive.

"You mentioned being here on business." Faith attempted to bring the subject around to less charged topics. "How is your airline company going?"

"Really well. I've just been operating with the one plane, with one other pilot besides myself, and an administrative assistant who does booking and some marketing work, but I'm about to expand," he said as he turned onto the highway.

"Really? That's wonderful, Ryan," Faith said enthusiastically. He'd mentioned to her casually while they talked at one of those Air Force picnics that he wanted to start up a charter airline business when he finally retired from the military. She'd been thrilled to hear when he paid her that unexpected Christmas Eve visit that he'd finally begun to live his dream. She was a little surprised at how gratifying it felt to her to know that Ryan was thriving and happy.

He gave her a sideways glance and smiled.

"Yeah. I've been flying a woman back and forth from this area to Lake Tahoe and San Francisco quite a bit—she has business to attend to in all those locations. Anyway, because I've been flying in and out of Tulip County Airport a lot because of this client, I've had my eye on a Cessna a man is selling there. I was going to make an offer on this visit. After I get a second plane, I'll be able to hire another pilot."

"That's great news," Faith said, even though her brain had gotten stuck on one thing that he'd said. "Tulip Country Airport is so close."

"Yeah. Only a few minutes from here."

"So...you've been back to this area several times in the past few months?"

He glanced at her, doing a double take when he saw her expression. "Yeah," he admitted.

Her pulse began to thrum at her throat. "Why did you only come to visit me today?"

He stared straight ahead at the road, but she sensed the tension that leapt into his muscles. "You told me last Christmas you didn't think we should see each other again."

"Well, I know," she said awkwardly. "But you came anyway. I was just wondering— why today?"

His jaw tightened. He didn't immediately

answer her, but focused on pulling into her office parking lot. Faith waited while he whipped the car concisely into a spot and put it into Park.

"I came because I'd hoped you'd had enough time to reconsider what you'd said that night," he said quietly. "Everything about what you told me today aside," he said, his gaze flickering down to her belly. "I was never convinced, like you seemed to be, that because of our…lapse, we should never see each other again. I came on that Christmas Eve to offer support to the widow of a good friend. Because it became more than that doesn't make it wrong."

Faith swallowed with difficulty, highly affected by the resonant timbre of his deep voice. An uneasy feeling settled in her belly. She shouldn't automatically assume that Ryan was like Jesse, but the only proof that she had was Jesse's joking, admiring references to the fact that Ryan could have just about any woman he wanted. He was in his mid to late thirties, and hadn't seemed to settle down into a monogamous relationship. After their all-too-brief encounter, she'd begun to wonder if he didn't consider sex in a similar vein to

Jesse. Jesse and Ryan were both handsome, dashing pilots—the type of men that made female hearts flutter across the globe.

That was what had been behind her insistence that what had happened between them was a mistake.

That, and his references to their impulsive lovemaking ruining the potential *friendship* he wanted with her.

She hadn't changed her mind in the past three months. It seemed a lot more difficult to bolster her logic, however, sitting just feet away from Ryan and inhaling his spicy male scent. The last thing Faith needed was to get involved with another faithless man—not that Ryan was interested. Besides, she had the baby to think about now.

"Faith, what are you thinking?" Ryan asked. She realized he must have seen the turmoil on her face.

"I still think it was a mistake what happened between us. Just because a baby is going to come of it doesn't mean we should continue going down that wrong road. I know that when you showed up at my house on Christmas Eve, you weren't thinking about

being strapped down with a woman and a baby."

"I'm not thinking of it as being *strapped down*," he said forcefully. "And just because I wasn't planning what happened doesn't automatically make it a mistake."

"I told you that I'm thrilled about the baby," she said sincerely. "It's a blessing to me. I've always wanted children. But the baby doesn't make it right for us to...*reconnect*, does it?"

He touched her jaw, the gesture in combination with his determined stare setting her off balance. His fingers felt warm and slightly calloused against her skin. She blinked in disorientation when he stroked the line of her jaw with his forefinger. "I think what's right is for us to spend more time together."

"Because of the baby?" she asked weakly.

His stare bored straight down into the core of her.

"No. Because I haven't been able to stop thinking about you since Christmas."

Chapter Two

Faith's pulse began to throb at her throat. She wanted to look away, but was ensnared by Ryan's eyes.

"Let me take you out to dinner tonight. We need to talk more," he said.

A battle waged in her breast. Part of her—the part that was getting breathless at the sensation of his skin touching her own—wanted very much to agree. Another part was wary, though. Her attraction for him could get her into a lot of trouble, and that was a potential heartache she'd already had enough of to last for three lifetimes.

Her practical side whispered to her that he only *couldn't stop thinking* about her since Christmas Eve because he felt guilty.

And yet she couldn't just ignore him. No matter how confused her feelings, Ryan was the father of her baby. Besides, she thought, breaking contact with his hand, there was a topic she really needed to broach with him.

"All right. As a matter of fact, there's something I want us to be on the same page about. It's about Jesse," she said.

He went still next to her, like a warrior suddenly sensing danger. "Okay," he replied slowly. "I suppose it's an inevitable topic, between us. Might as well face it head-on."

She gave him a puzzled glance.

"I just mean that Jesse's the common denominator between us." He hesitated. Faith had the impression he was choosing his words very carefully. "He must be on your mind a lot. That's understandable, especially now that…" He glanced briefly at her stomach and then out the front window. His jaw tightened.

Her heart went out to him. She knew from some of the things he'd said on Christmas Eve that he'd considered his actions to be the worst sort of treachery toward a friend.

It didn't matter to him that Jesse had been dead for almost a year when they'd gotten together. Anger splintered through her at the thought. Jesse didn't deserve Ryan's show of loyalty. Not when Jesse himself had been so faithless.

"The baby has nothing to do with Jesse, Ryan," she said coolly, reaching for the door handle. "That's not what I wanted to talk to you about."

He put his hand on her shoulder, halting her exit. For a few seconds she thought he was going to demand that she tell him what she'd meant.

"I'll stop by your house tonight. Say six?" he said instead.

She nodded once, willfully ignoring her heart pounding in her ears, and stepped out of the car.

Ryan watched her through the window as she walked toward her office. Her figure still looked graceful and slender—from the back, anyway. He hadn't been able to stop himself from noticing as they sat in the car, however, that her breasts appeared fuller than he recalled beneath the fitted, belted jacket she wore. His thoughts strayed to what she'd felt like on that night—petal-soft, exquisitely sensitive skin sliding beneath his fingertips... his lips.

The sound of the office door shutting behind Faith made him blink. His erotic memories scattered. What was he doing, sitting here fantasizing about Faith when he'd just gotten some of the most shocking, amazing news of his life?

His mind went over their conversation. He'd wondered incessantly if Faith knew about Jesse's womanizing. Something about her tension-filled reference to Jesse just now had sent a warning bell going off in his head. Was Faith planning to tell him that Jesse would forever be the love of her life, that she deeply regretted their volatile, unexpected lovemaking?

Or was she going to tell him that she knew about Jesse's infidelities?

Damn.

He didn't know which possible truth pained him more. He dreaded the possibility of hearing that Faith would eternally be loyal to a man who was gone. He despised the idea of how much Faith would have suffered at the knowledge that Jesse had been unfaithful to her.

He took a moment to try to absorb everything that had happened to him in the past few hours. No matter how hard he tried, he couldn't do it.

Faith was going to have a baby, and he was the father.

She planned to raise the child here in Michigan, thousands of miles from where he worked and lived.

Being that far away suddenly become a reality he couldn't bear.

It was bizarre to realize that just last Christmas, his sister Mari had announced she was going to have another baby. Until a few years ago Mari had been Ryan's only living family. Mari and her husband Marc Kavanaugh had had a daughter, and Ryan had felt blessed to add another name to the family list. Soon, he'd have another family member. It'd been amazing news to receive, even if there had been a hint of sadness mixing with his jubilation. He was thrilled for Mari, of course, but hearing about her pregnancy had made him wonder if he'd ever experience the same joy firsthand. Romance and women had come easily to him. Finding someone with whom he wanted to spend the rest of his life and build a family had proved to be much more elusive.

Strange, to consider in retrospect, that the same night Mari had announced she was going to have another baby, he'd driven the twenty miles from Harbor Town to Faith's house and done the unthinkable. He'd created his own.

He'd beaten himself up for losing control that night, but Faith had been so lovely, so fresh…so sweet. Had his admiration for her just been the surface of a much deeper attraction, feelings that had to be repressed given her marriage to his good friend?

He suspected that was the case. The only thing he knew for certain, Ryan thought grimly as he turned the ignition, was that there had been an inevitable quality to what they'd done on Christmas Eve. There was no changing it now. He wasn't sure he would, even if he could.

Instead of pulling out of the parking lot, he dialed a number on his cell phone.

"Deidre? It's Ryan," he said when Deidre Kavanaugh Malone, the client he'd flown to southwestern Michigan answered. Deidre was technically more than a client; she was extended family. Her brother Marc was married to Ryan's sister, Mari. He'd known Deidre since they were kids spending their idyllic summers in Harbor Town. Deidre had recently inherited a large fortune and was currently one of the wealthiest women in the country, but she remained the friendly, brave girl he'd always known.

Several months ago, Deidre and Nick Malone, the CEO of DuBois Enterprises, had set the business and social world ablaze with the news of their marriage. The financial world had assumed that Deidre and Nick, co-owner and leader of the DuBois conglomerate, would be natural adversaries. As an insider and friend to the couple, however, Ryan knew that immense wealth, media speculation and glitz and glamour aside, Deidre and Nick were deeply devoted to one another.

"Hi, what's up?" she asked.

"If it's all right with you, I'm going to have Scott fly in commercial to take you back to Lake Tahoe in a few days," he said, referring to Scott Mason, the other pilot that worked for his company, Eagle Air.

"That's fine with me," Deidre replied. "But is everything all right?"

"Yeah. I just got some news that is going to make it necessary to spend more time here in Michigan."

"Good or bad news?"

Ryan considered the question as he put the car in Reverse.

"Shocking…confusing…but good," he said. "Definitely good."

"I can't wait to hear about it."

"You will, eventually. It's not the kind of news that can stay a secret for long," he said dryly before he said his goodbye.

At six that evening Faith smoothed the black skirt over her hips and turned to examine herself in profile in the bathroom mirror. She hadn't gained a single pound so far with her pregnancy, something that her obstetrician insisted was perfectly normal for the end of the first trimester. Nevertheless her body weight seemed to be redistributing. There was a subtle curve to her once-flat belly and her breasts were starting to threaten to burst out of her bras. Faith kept having the strangest sensation that she was transforming...blooming like a flower.

She heard a knock at her front door. Topsy, her new puppy, began to yap loudly from the utility room. Her reflection in the mirror had previously been rosy-cheeked in anxious anticipation at going to dinner with Ryan. At the sound of his knock all of the color drained away.

She left the bathroom and hurried down the hallway to the front door. She couldn't help but relive racing toward the front door to greet him on Christmas Eve. Tonight's anxiety was worse, though. Much worse.

She swung open the front door. "Hi," she greeted upon seeing his tall, broad shouldered shadow on her stoop. "Come on in. I'm sorry about the racket."

"You got a dog?" Ryan asked, stepping into the foyer. Faith backed up, making room for him.

"Yes. A few weeks ago," she said, switching on the foyer light. For a split second they both examined each other. Faith blushed. Was he, too, recalling the other time he'd entered her house and they'd stood in this exact spot, inspecting each other with a sort of breathless curiosity? He looked fantastic—male and rugged, wearing a pair of jeans that emphasized his long legs and narrow hips, a white shirt and a worn dark brown leather flight jacket.

"You look great," he said.

"Thanks. You like nice, too," Faith murmured, feeling embarrassed. She'd worried she'd overdressed in the black skirt, leather boots and forest-green sweater. They weren't going on a *date,* after all. Despite that, she hadn't been able to stop herself from taking extra time with her grooming, even spending the ridiculous amount of time it took to straighten her hair with a flatiron.

She waved toward the interior of the house. "I just have to put Topsy in her crate, and I'll be ready to go."

"Topsy?" he asked, and she realized he was following her. She glanced over her shoulder.

"Yes, she was the runt of the litter from one of my oldest patients, a golden retriever named Erica," Faith explained breathlessly as they walked through the dining room and entered the kitchen. "All of Erica's purebred puppies went like hotcakes, but we had more trouble finding homes for this litter. Erica had an unexpected love affair with a local playboy—a spaniel-poodle mix. I was able to find homes for all of Topsy's brothers and sisters, but poor Topsy remained unclaimed."

"And so you couldn't resist adopting him... *her*?"

"Yes. Topsy's a she."

"You told me on Christmas Eve that you had a *strict* rule about pet adoption."

Faith paused next to the gaited entryway to the utility room. She blinked when she saw Ryan's mouth curved in a grin, his gaze warm on her face.

"If I took in every patient who needs a home that comes through my practice I'd be out of a home myself," she said.

Ryan didn't speak, just continued to study her with that knowing, sexy smile. Topsy yapped impatiently behind her.

Faith sighed and shrugged sheepishly. Ryan had her number, all right. "Well, I had a moment of weakness when I looked into Topsy's brown eyes. And like I told you," she said, her cheeks turning warmer even at the memory of their former meeting here in this house, "I had to take in Cleo—she's diabetic, and I couldn't convince anyone to do her injections every day. Smokey doesn't count, either, because who wouldn't give a home to a little thing like that?" Faith said, waving at the three-legged, pale gray cat that hobbled fleetly into the kitchen after them.

"There's no reason to be apologetic because you have a kind heart," he said quietly. He glanced down to his feet when Smokey brushed against his ankles. He bent and stroked the affectionate feline. Faith had been so offset by his candid compliment that she was glad for the interruption.

"Are you still serving as the president of the Animal Advocates Alliance?" he asked a moment later, standing.

"Oh, yes," Faith said enthusiastically, glad for a safer topic. Ryan knew about her charity work from Jesse. She'd been extremely touched when he'd made a generous donation to both the Armed Forces Foundation and the Animal Advocates Alliance in Jesse's name following the chopper crash that had killed him. She unhooked the gate that kept Topsy in the utility room. "The annual fundraiser ball is next week. I put a lot of hard work into it. Well?" she asked, glancing back at him. "Would you like to meet the Queen of Cute?"

"I can't wait," he said, walking toward her.

She started to open the gate wide enough for both of them to squeeze into the utility room without releasing the excited puppy, but noticed Ryan stared at her back door.

"What happened here?" he asked, pausing to look at the improvised "lock"—a thick piece of wood nailed to each side of the door. His eyebrows slanted in worry. "Nobody tried to break in, did they?"

"Oh, no. It's nothing. The old lock came loose, and I haven't had a chance to hire a locksmith to come and replace it yet." She shrugged. "It's not very pretty, but it'll keep things out. I've had a real rush of patients at my office as the weather warms up, and I just haven't had a chance to get it fixed."

"I'll come and put a lock on it tomorrow."

"Ryan, that's not necessary," she said, set off balance by his steadfast offer.

"It's not a big deal." Instead of waiting for her to inch back the gate—or to protest his offer—he just stepped over it.

"Hi, Topsy," he said.

Topsy wiggled in irrepressible excitement. She looked like a caramel-colored powder puff.

"I introduce you to Her Highness, Topsy-Turvy Blackwell."

"I was hoping she'd be a little bigger," he said.

"Oh, she'll still grow quite a bit."

"Yeah, but she doesn't look like she'll ever be much of a watchdog, does she?" he asked dubiously. He noticed her equally confused expression. "It is awfully isolated out here on this road."

He was obviously worried about the baby, Faith realized. "It's very safe here in the country, Ryan. I grew up in this house, and we've never had any problems. This area has one of the lowest crime rates in the state. It's quite safe and close to the population I serve, as well. Lots of my patients live on farms hereabouts."

Ryan didn't seem entirely convinced, but he refrained from disagreeing with her. Instead he bent his tall frame to pet the vibrating puppy. "How come you named her Topsy-Turvy *Blackwell*?"

"Oh. It's my maiden name. I plan to use it again, I just haven't gotten around to having it legally changed yet."

He looked up, his eyelids narrowing on her.

She felt x-rayed. "I see," he said quietly, resuming petting Topsy.

"Do you?" Faith asked cautiously.

He didn't answer for a moment as he stroked the wriggling puppy. "I think I do. That's what you wanted to talk to me about tonight, isn't it?"

Faith swallowed thickly. A heavy sensation pressed down on her chest. Ryan knew that Jesse had been unfaithful to her. How else to explain his shuttered gaze and apparent discomfort? She experienced a wilting sensation. It was illogical and stupid, she knew, but it shamed her, to suspect he knew of Jesse's infidelities. No matter how much she rationally knew that Jesse had been in the wrong, she still felt vaguely substandard as a female, knowing he'd found other women more exciting than her, that she hadn't been sufficiently worth it for him to deny temptation and remain faithful.

"Yes, it is what I wanted to discuss with you. Among other things," she admitted, glancing away from his stare.

He nodded once and stood. "I guess we better get going, then."

She agreed. He helped her to put the squirming puppy into the crate.

"Topsy may not be ferocious, but you were right. She's the cutest thing I've ever laid eyes on," he observed a moment later as he opened the front door for her. Faith damned her pounding heart when he casually touched her waist as they walked together to his car.

"What are you hungry for?" she asked a few seconds later when he backed out of her driveway onto the rural road.

"I've already made reservations for dinner at Butch's Dry Dock, downtown." He glanced in her direction when she didn't immediately respond. "Is that all right?"

"Oh…yes," she said, flustered. "I love Butch's."

She couldn't tell him his response had set her off guard because he'd planned dinner with her at one of the nicest restaurants in the area. Despite her self-admonishments to remember that this was an opportunity to settle business with the father of her baby, the evening was, indeed, starting to feel more and more like a date.

An hour later Faith watched as Ryan leaned against the high-backed booth at Butch's, the remains of their delicious meal still on the table. Ryan had seemed intent on making her comfortable during their dinner, and his efforts were paying off. Her nervousness had slowly faded as the meal progressed and Ryan regaled her with some inevitable funny mistakes he'd made in starting up his business from scratch. It suddenly struck her that they hadn't yet landed on the topic of Jesse. She wondered if Ryan was avoiding the issue purposefully.

"Can I ask you a personal question?" Ryan asked, his eyes warm on her.

"It depends," she said, a smile flickering across her mouth.

"What's it been like for you? Being pregnant?"

"Oh," she said, her eyes going wide. "It's been…nice."

"You haven't been getting sick or anything?"

She nodded. "Yes, I got nauseous almost every day around the seven week mark, but believe it or not, I never threw up. It usually faded when I ate some crackers. I just had to make sure I didn't let my stomach get empty. It's gotten much better in the past week."

"And fatigue?"

Again, she nodded, this time more emphatically. She paused while a busboy came to clear their table. "That was probably the worst of it." She resumed when they were alone again. "Once I figured out why I felt like taking a nap by ten o'clock every morning, it seemed to help things, though."

"When did you find out? That you were pregnant?" he asked.

"When I was about five weeks along."

"I wish you would have called me."

The back of her neck prickled with awareness at the sound of his low, resonant voice.

"I meant to tell you all along, Ryan. Please believe that. I was going to tell you at the same time I told my parents."

"I believe you. You're much too honest to make me think otherwise."

She gave him a thankful smile. "I just wanted to get through my first trimester safely."

"I understand," he said. She searched his face. Seeing not a hint of anger, she sighed in relief.

"Ryan, there's something I want us to be on the same page about," she approached the topic cautiously after the waiter brought them coffee and tea. She sensed the tension that flew into his muscles.

"About Jesse?" he asked.

She nodded, took a deep breath for courage and blurted out the details of discovering Jesse's infidelities. She was learning to read him, she realized after a minute or two of talking almost nonstop. Most people would have called his flat expression impassive, but that slight widening of his eyes meant all-out shock on Ryan's face.

"I can't believe it," he said. "Melanie Shane *contacted* you, and told you about her affair with your husband?"

Faith nodded and poured hot water over her tea bag. The pain that went through her at the vivid memory was lessening now, altering from the stab of betrayal to the ache of regret. Mostly she was mad at herself for not facing the truth earlier. Jesse was charming and funny and dynamic, but he was *not* a one-woman man.

Nor a two-woman man, for that matter.

Sometimes it was just easier to be blind to the obvious.

"It was a few months before the crash. She found me through my veterinary practice's website," she said. She set down her spoon and met Ryan's stare. "I'm just thankful that I happened to open the emails that morning. Often, Jane does it before me."

Ryan shut his eyes briefly. Pain flickered across his hard face and was gone. "They had the most volatile relationship. Jesse and Melanie were either fighting like cats and dogs or they were—"

He stopped abruptly. Their stares held as she finished his sentence in her mind.

"When Melanie first wrote me, she was in quite a state," Faith said after a long pause. "Apparently she'd discovered that Jesse had slept with a lieutenant who trained airmen on computers at the airport. Melanie was pretty upset by it."

Ryan grimaced. "Damn. I can't believe Melanie did that." He exhaled heavily. "Strike that. I can. She'd get herself into a real state at times, when it came to Jesse. I suppose she had herself convinced she was doing you a favor by pouncing on you with the news?"

Faith nodded. "Bingo. You'd think we were blood sisters, both betrayed by the devil."

Ryan grunted. "When in reality, Melanie was feeling furious and rejected by what

Jesse had done. She ran blabbing to you because she knew it would hurt Jesse. She never gave a thought or care about what she was doing to you. I'm sorry, Faith."

"It's not your fault. You have nothing to apologize for."

A muscle flickered subtly in his cheek. She shook her head sadly.

"You are *not* responsible for Jesse's actions," she stated the obvious.

"I'm responsible for my own."

Faith swallowed uneasily. Is that how he thought of her and the baby? A responsibility? A burden?

"What was Melanie like?" she asked shakily after a moment, trying to divert his attention.

Ryan shrugged and poured some cream into his coffee. "A good chopper pilot. Volatile. Bit of a daredevil. Feisty exterior with a vulnerable core," he mumbled succinctly.

"She was...pretty?"

He glanced up, pausing in the action of setting down the small pitcher. "Some men might have found her attractive," he said with what struck Faith as forced neutrality.

She stared at the snowy-white tablecloth.

Much to her surprise, given the topic, she wasn't that upset. She'd suspected all along she wasn't as devastated by the news as she should have been that Jesse was unfaithful. She'd been hurt. Jesse had been her husband, after all, and she'd planned to spend the rest of her life with him—before she'd discovered his infidelities.

But deep down she knew that if Jessie'd been the love of her life, that email from Melanie—and Jesse's eventual admission that Melanie's accusations were valid—wouldn't have just been an unpleasant shock. It would have been a lancing, debilitating blow to her spirit.

Jesse had been so full of life. She'd often reflected after she'd learned of his infidelity that she didn't want to be Jesse's wife anymore, but she would have wished him well. Always. It hurt, to think of him not out there in the world somewhere…raising hell, warming someone with his smile and his jokes, hopefully finding the happiness she couldn't give him.

She became aware of Ryan's gaze on her—warm, concerned, wary. So, he *had* known all along about Jesse's womanizing. How did that knowledge factor into their impulsive, impassioned tryst on Christmas Eve? How would it play into the fact that they were going to have a baby together? It was becoming increasingly clear that Ryan felt some sort of misguided responsibility toward her.

"Don't pity me," she said.

"I don't pity you," he said, his eyebrows pinching together in apparent bewilderment at her quiet forcefulness.

"No?" she asked, calmly removing the chamomile teabag from her cup. "You don't have some kind of knight in shining armor syndrome going on for the scorned wife? You said that you visited me last Christmas Eve because you wanted to make sure I was okay…safe. Now that I'm pregnant, I don't want you feeling regretful, Ryan. I need a father for my baby, not a guilty lover. I don't want you to feel sorry for me."

The spoon he'd been using to stir his coffee fell several inches to the saucer with a loud clinking sound. "That's insulting."

She met his stare levelly, difficult though it was. His eyes blazed like black fire. "Then why did you act so guilty about Christmas Eve? I'm not the fragile victim you're imagining. If that was part of the appeal that night, you were misguided," she said quietly.

He placed his forearms on the table and leaned toward her, his nostrils slightly flared. "I didn't *know* whether or not you knew about Jesse and Melanie on Christmas Eve. For all I knew, you were still grieving the love of your life. I wanted you so much, I went ahead and did what I did anyway. So much for the idea that I'm *pitying* you."

The anger clinging thickly to Ryan's words didn't have quite the effect on her that she would have thought. For some reason, the memory of their fevered joining chose that moment to bombard her consciousness like rapid-fire bullets—Ryan's hands moving over her in carnal worship, his mouth closing over the tip of her breast and the answering sharp pain of longing in her womb, the feeling of him filling her until she was inundated by him, ready to burst with her desire.

By slow degrees she became aware that the blend of voices and clanking cutlery and china had become a distant buzz in her ears. Ryan blinked as if awakening from a trance and sat back in the booth.

"I am far from thinking that you're a weak

victim." His gaze flickered up to meet hers. "I like you. I have from the first time Jesse ever read me one of your letters. I liked you even more when I finally met you. I respect the way you've built up your business and your life, even though you were a military wife and alone a lot of the time. I admired how you always managed to be so cheerful...convey so much warmth. I used to get resentful when Jesse didn't return your letters regularly. I used to get resentful toward Jesse for a lot of things," he mumbled under his breath, looking angry...*torn.*

"Can I bring you any dessert?"

Both of them blinked and stared at the waiter like he was an alien.

"Faith?" Ryan asked.

"No, nothing for me," Faith said.

Ryan also declined and the waiter left. Faith took a long drink of her ice water.

"That all still sounds like you're feeling sorry for me, Ryan," she said shakily.

"I don't pity you, but I do feel bad about some things that have happened," he said quietly. "I feel like a heel for barging in on you and laying you down on a couch and having unprotected sex with you after I'd been in your house for all of a half hour."

Her mouth fell open at his blunt words. Once again the remembered images and sensations swamped her awareness.

"Let me get this straight," she said slowly. "You like me, and you respect me, but because you wanted to have sex with me that night, that's a problem. Is that because you usually don't like and respect the women you sleep with? Attraction and respect don't go together in your mind?"

"That's a hell of a thing to say."

"Jesse used to imply that you liked female companionship, but weren't much for a serious relationship with one woman."

Realization subtly settled on his features. His eyelids narrowed. Faith caught an edge of the diamond-hard focus that had made him such a valuable officer and pilot. "Are you implying I'm like Jesse?"

She tilted her chin up, refusing to be intimidated. "Maybe."

"Well I'm not," he stated flatly. "I'm not saying Christmas Eve was a mistake because I'm a womanizer. I'm saying it was a mistake because it was so abrupt…strange…ir-rational…"

Mind-blowing, Faith added in her private thoughts. His gaze flickered up to meet hers, as if she'd spoken aloud.

After a tense moment she exhaled and sagged in the seat. "I'm sorry. It's not my place to judge you one way or another. That part of your life is none of my business."

She glanced up in surprise when he reached across the table and grasped her hand.

"Just because I haven't found the right woman yet doesn't mean I haven't been look-ing. I don't thrive on conquest. Christmas Eve was *not* about that."

She couldn't look away from his eyes. His hand tightened on hers, his fingers brushing her wrist. She wondered distantly if he could feel the throb of her pulse.

"What was it about then?" she whispered.

Something flickered across his rugged fea-tures she couldn't quite identify. "I'm not en-tirely sure. It just felt…unstoppable. Like I said that night, all that emotion must have been building."

"You do hear about it happening after a

tragic death," Faith admitted. "Stuff builds up and then…bang. A lightning strike."

They stared at each other across the table. Was he, like her, recalling what it'd been like as the electric desire blazed in their flesh, enlivened them, fused them?

"We're going to have a baby together," he said. "All of my life is your business now. Fate has seen to that. Whether we planned it or not, whether you like it or not, we're family now, Faith."

Chapter Three

When they walked out onto Eighth Street
later, the sun was setting.

"How about a drive? There are a few things
I'd still like to talk to you about," Ryan added
when she gave him a doubtful sideways glance.
He's sensed her wariness ever since he'd said
that thing about them being family.

"Okay," Faith replied, although she looked
uncertain.

He grabbed her hand and gave it a small
squeeze as they walked toward his car. He
waited for her to look at him.

"Why are you so uncomfortable around

me? Is it just because of the baby?" he couldn't help but ask.

"You're not entirely comfortable around me, either, Ryan. I think we both know this situation is…unusual."

He grimaced slightly. He'd been more than a little confused about his feelings for Faith for a long time now. Finding out she was carrying his baby only amplified his bewilderment along with a lot of other emotions.

He'd never been able to tell anyone he had a sort of secret…*thing* for Jesse's wife for years now. It was too mild to be a crush. Ryan had secretly found his partiality for news about Faith or hearing her letters a little amusing in a self-deprecating sort of way. His feelings for her had never gone anywhere beyond admiration.

But as he drove through picturesque downtown Holland with Faith in the seat next to him, he'd have to admit it in hindsight that he'd been a little envious of Jesse for having a wife like Faith. It wasn't just that Faith was beautiful in the natural, girl-next-door, very sexy kind of way. He was drawn to her freshness, her intelligence, and most of all, her kindness.

He'd been highly irritated at Jesse for proving time and again that he didn't deserve her.

The fact of the matter was, until Christmas Eve, he'd never given his admiration for her much thought. She'd been off-limits for almost the entire time he'd known her. Maybe Jesse wasn't the ideal husband, and perhaps Ryan had questioned his judgment as an officer for getting involved with women during deployments, but Jesse had never done anything overtly to make Ryan question his ability to do his job. As a matter of fact Jesse had been a fine pilot, and in the friendship department at least, loyal to the bone.

The sun blazed bright orange, about to make its fiery plunge into the silvery waters of Lake Michigan when Ryan pulled the car into a lot at Laketown Beach. Because of the dunes, they were on a high vista. The beach itself was at the bottom of a long staircase. He shut off the ignition and glanced at Faith. He found the black leather, calf-hugging boots she wore extremely sexy, but wasn't so sure the heels were walking-friendly.

"There's a paved path along the bluff. Are you up for a walk?"

"Yes," she agreed.

She smiled at him a moment later when he came around the car to meet her. "I know you spent your summers in Harbor Town, but you seem very familiar with Holland, too."

He shrugged as he zipped up his jacket. There was a cool breeze coming off Lake Michigan. "My mom and dad used to bring us to Holland occasionally for dinner or a day at the beach."

"I think you said your parents have passed?" she asked softly. He recalled he'd mentioned to her that his parents were no longer living at one of those Air Force picnics, but hadn't given her any details.

"Yeah. They died while I was still at the Air Force Academy in Colorado. Dad used to like to explore the area when he'd come down on the weekends from Dearborn, so Mari— that's my sister—and I have seen pretty much every beach on the Michigan shoreline. I've done some exploring on my own in Holland for the past couple months, though," he said as he took her hand and they made their way down the sidewalk that trailed along the edge of the bluff. "When Deidre comes in for an overnight visit, I stay at a hotel near the airport."

"Deidre is the client you fly to this area?"

"Yeah, Deidre Kavanaugh Malone. When we were kids, the Kavanaughs lived on the same street as us in Harbor Town."

He glanced around in surprise when Faith suddenly came to an abrupt halt.

"Deidre's not *Brigit* Kavanaugh's daughter, is she?" Faith asked.

"Yeah. Faith?" he prompted, slightly alarmed when he saw her flattened expression.

"But that means... Ryan, was it your *parents* that were killed in that terrible car wreck all those years ago?"

Ryan inhaled slowly. "Yeah. How did you know?"

"I know Brigit Kavanaugh."

"How?"

"She's a member of the Southwestern Michigan's Women's Auxiliary. It's one of their missions to offer deployed military family members support. She came to visit me after Jesse died last year, and we've become friends." He saw Faith's throat tighten as she swallowed. Her face looked stricken. "She told me about her husband getting drunk and causing that accident. She told me that a couple had been killed that had lived just down the street from her. Oh, Ryan," she finished in a whisper. Tears filled her green eyes. "I'm so sorry. We heard about that crash here in Holland when I was a teenager, but I didn't recall any specific details. Brigit never mentioned names. I never realized...your *parents*."

"It's okay, Faith," he said, concerned by her pale cheeks and obvious distress. He didn't have to think twice about taking her into his arms. She came willingly, hugging his waist as if to give him comfort. He lowered his head and pressed his mouth to her hair. He inhaled the achingly familiar scent of citrus and flowers. "It happened a long time ago," he murmured, lifting his head and willing her to look up at him. When she did, he used his thumb to gently wipe off several tears from her cheek.

"But you and your sister were so young. Did you have other family?"

"Only an aunt in San Francisco," Ryan murmured distractedly as he continued to touch her cheek. Her skin was incredibly smooth and soft. "She passed away a few years ago, though."

"I'm so sorry, Ryan," she said in a choked voice.

His heart squeezed a little in his chest. She seemed genuinely pained by the news that his parents had passed away almost seventeen years ago. He stopped drying her cheeks and palmed her delicate jaw.

"You're an amazingly nice woman, do you know that, Faith? Jesse never deserved you."

She blinked. Ryan realized how intense he'd just sounded. He hadn't meant to speak his thoughts out loud, but seeing Faith's lovely, troubled face and experiencing her compassion had caused the words to pop out of his throat. He regretted it when she released her hold on him and took a step back. A lake breeze whipped past them and Faith tightened the belt on her coat.

"Maybe we ought to skip the walk," Ryan said.

"No. No, let's walk over to that bench and watch the sunset," she said. "It's funny," she said a moment later as they sat side by side on the wooden bench next to the path. "I grew up watching these sunsets, but I never get tired of them."

"Kind of hard to get tired of something like that," Ryan agreed. For a few seconds they both watched silently as the ball of fire began to dip below the horizon, shades of magenta, pink and gold splashing across the sky in its wake.

"It's not too hard to believe you're pregnant," he said, studying her delicate, lovely face cast in the pink and gold shades of the sunset. Her face didn't "glow" like the stereotypical pregnant woman, but there was a sort of soft luminescence to her that he found compelling. "You've never looked so beautiful."

The pink in her cheeks wasn't caused by the sunset, he realized. Another breeze whipped past them, this one chillier. He leaned back on the bench and put his arm around her. Much to his satisfaction, she let her head rest on his shoulder. For several seconds they watched the sunset in silence. He felt entirely aware of her in those moments, of her firm, curving body, of her sweetness, the scent of her hair, the lock that fell just next to the pulse at her white throat. He brushed away the lock, stroking her skin in the process. Her shiver vibrated into his flesh. He braced himself for her reaction to what he was about to say.

"I can't leave you alone here, Faith," he said gruffly.

She lifted her head and studied him dazedly. "What do you mean?"

"I respect the fact that you want to raise the baby in Holland. It's your home. But I'm not comfortable with living three thousand miles away while my child is here."

Regret swept through him when he saw alarm flash into her eyes. She straightened, breaking the contact of their bodies.

"What do you plan to do?" she demanded.

"I'll move back to Michigan," he replied simply.

She blinked. "Ryan, you can't be serious. You've lived in San Francisco for years now. You started your new business out there. You can't expect to just pack up and move to Holland."

"It'll take some doing, I'll grant you that. But it'd be better to do it now, before the business grows any larger. I can even rent hangar space at Tulip County Airport. I've been giving it a lot of thought since this afternoon. It might be better for me to be centrally located versus on the West Coast, given the nature of my business. Actually, the beach area of Michigan is an ideal location to serve business people in Detroit and Chicago, and I've already make loads of contacts out west."

Faith stared at him like he was slightly mad as he spoke his thoughts out loud. "Ryan, that seems so…sudden. Impulsive."

"Despite all the evidence against me from Christmas Eve, I'm not an impulsive person. But I do trust my instincts." He traced the line of her jaw with his forefinger.

She met his stare. He didn't bother to guard his desire for her. Her eyes widened slightly, and he knew she'd seen it. Was she, like him, thinking of those ecstatic moments when they'd both acted on glorious instinct? He hoped so. He wished like hell those memories had been permanently scored in her brain like they had been in his.

"I think we should talk about it more," she said in a voice barely above a whisper. "I'm not so sure instinct is the wise guiding principle for the future, given the fact that a baby is involved."

"I think it's the perfect principle."

"Why do you say that?"

"It got us here, didn't it?"

She stared at him in mute amazement.

Ryan scowled at the sound of voices in the

distance. He turned his head and saw another couple approaching on the walk.

"Come on. It's almost dark," he said. "We can talk more in the car."

Faith's mind was a confused hodgepodge of thoughts, feelings and concerns as Ryan drove through the now dark streets of Holland. While they waited at a red light, Ryan turned toward her.

"You're vibrating with worry over there. Why don't you vent some of what you're thinking?"

She met his stare. His rugged features looked shadowed and compelling in the dim light.

"Are you really serious about moving back to Michigan?" she asked in a voice that sounded unnaturally high to her own ears.

"Is it really that unbelievable?"

"I just… I just hadn't expected that you might want to do that."

"Why not?" he asked, looking slightly puzzled. The stoplight turned green and he began to drive. "Did you really think I was going to be blasé about the fact that I was going to have a child?"

"I don't know," Faith stated honestly. "I guess I just assumed you'd…"

"Be satisfied seeing the baby a few times a month and on half the holidays?" Ryan asked when she faded off uncertainly.

"Well…you're a pilot," she said, as if that explained something.

"And?"

"Pilots are always on the go. One place is as much home as another. I just assumed you wouldn't consider the distance between Holland and San Francisco as significant as most people would."

He came to a stop at an intersection of a quiet residential neighborhood. "Family is very important to me, Faith. It always has been. That value was instilled into me a long time ago by my parents."

Her throat grew tight. "And then you lost them at such a young age," she whispered feelingly. Of course family was important to him.

"Besides, if I move back to Michigan, I'll be closer to my sister and her family. Mari is in Chicago. She's going to have another baby, too." He blinked as if in realization and gave her a small smile. Her heart seemed to throb as if in answer. "As a matter of fact, she's only a few months ahead of you."

"The baby will like having a cousin of the same age," Faith said, returning his smile.

The moment stretched as they sat there in the running car in the silent neighborhood, staring at one another and considering the future.

Ryan finally cleared his throat and resumed driving.

"You never told me if you knew the sex of the baby," he said.

She shook her head. "Not yet. I hadn't decided yet if I wanted to know or be surprised. Do you?" He glanced at her quickly. "Want to know?"

She watched as his expression went blank. He looked almost grim as he stared out the front window.

"I don't know," he said hoarsely after a moment. "One second, I think this whole thing has settled in, and the next I feel..."

"Overwhelmed?" she wondered.

He nodded once.

"I understand. It takes a while to fully absorb it," she said quietly. She studied his profile as he drove, wondering over the fact that she was sitting in the car with Ryan Itani—her former husband's good friend, the father of the child that grew in her womb…one of the most magnetically attractive and masculine men she'd ever encountered.

Maybe she was still overwhelmed, as well.

He pulled into her driveway a few minutes later. Faith studied her hands in her lap as he put the car in Park. She needed to banish this pervasive nervousness. She needed to get used to dealing with Ryan, with being around him.

"Would you like to come in and have a cup of coffee?"

"Yes." The bluntness of his reply made her head come up. In the dim dashboard lights, she could see him studying her. "But I'm going to say no, nevertheless," he added.

"Why?"

He abruptly turned in the seat as far as he could, given his big body and the confining space of the car. He took both of her hands in his. Spikes of pleasure prickled up her arms when he caressed her wrists with slightly calloused thumbs.

"I still want you, Faith. I think it's only fair to tell you that."

She started, shocked by his bold statement. She stared out the window to her neat, attractive ranch house, trying to gather her thoughts. It was hard with him stroking her skin and what he'd just said echoing around in her brain. She reached wildly for the threads of logic spinning around with a vortex of doubts and desire.

"You're just saying that because you're confused about the baby," she said.

"You said I was saying it last time because I was confused about Jesse's sudden death. When are you going to believe that I've always found you attractive, Faith?"

She looked at him in alarm.

"I never would have done anything while Jesse was alive. That's not my style. I know it's not yours, either," he said in a low, compelling voice. "The truth is, I didn't allow myself to think about it very much. You were another man's wife. Off-limits. I wouldn't even call my feelings toward you attraction. They were respect. Admiration. I liked you a lot."

She stared at him, her throat and chest feeling full—achy. She couldn't look away from his stark, handsome face.

"My feelings for you would have stayed in that holding pattern if circumstances hadn't changed. But they *did* change. You discovered Jesse wasn't faithful to you."

"I was filing for a divorce at the time he was killed," she said, shocking herself.

Ryan's expression tensed. His caressing fingers paused. "You were?"

She nodded. A tear spilled down her cheek. She was angry at Jesse for his infidelity. Furious. So why did guilt still rear its ugly head inside her when she thought of the fact that she'd been planning on leaving him when his life was cut unexpectedly short?

"I told him that I planned to divorce him when he admitted to his affairs with both Melanie and that other officer that worked at the airport. He was so upset about the divorce. He never told you?" she asked shakily, searching his face.

"He never said a word about you two breaking up," Ryan said. His flat expression told the absolute truth. Jesse had kept the impending end of their marriage to himself. Maybe he'd hoped she'd change her mind. He might have died with that secret. The realization caused a pain of regret to go through her. She shuddered. Damn these hormones. Since her pregnancy, she cried at the drop of a dime. Suddenly Ryan's arms were around her. She clutched on to his shoulders and wept.

"It's just...you knew Jesse. He was like a kid at times. I know he wasn't capable of being faithful. I know I wasn't meant to be his wife. But I cared about him."

"I understand," Ryan soothed, stroking her back. "Maybe he wasn't capable of being faithful to you, but I do know that Jesse cared about you, too."

"I hate to think of him dying, knowing that I was leaving him," Faith managed between bitter tears.

"I'm sure he was feeling regretful about having hurt you."

That made her sob harder.

"I'm sorry," he said, stroking her arms and back. "I shouldn't have said that."

"No. No, it's true. I suppose some people would feel vindicated that he felt guilty on the day he died, but I think it's just..."

"Terrible," Ryan finished for her. "I understand."

"Do you?" she asked wetly, leaning back slightly in order to see his face. His features looked like they'd been carved from rock in the dim lights emanating from the dashboard.

"Yeah. I think we both know that while Jesse might not have been ideal husband material, he was a good guy in a lot of other areas of life. It's got to be hard for you, thinking of him dying knowing that he'd done you wrong."

"Exactly," she whispered shakily.

"It's still not your fault, Faith. You didn't do anything wrong. You had every right to file for divorce once you learned he'd cheated on you, not once, but several times. It's just that life took a rotten turn in the interim, and Jesse was killed. You have absolutely nothing to feel guilty about."

"I know," she said weakly. She touched the side of his neck along his hairline. His hair was a pleasure to her fingertips—crisp and soft at once. "I'm always telling myself I didn't do anything wrong. I just wish I hadn't told him about the divorce when he was about to…"

Ryan shook his head, his face now rigid with compassion. "You're not all-seeing." He cradled her jaw gently. She went still, utterly aware of the intimate contact. "Death is the same way. You can't beat yourself up for things you don't have any control over. All we can do is take what we've been given and make the best of it."

His breath was warm and fragrant against her upturned lips and nose.

"I want to make the best of *this*, Faith—for whatever is happening between you and me," he said, his voice like a rough caress. "Part of me feels guilty for making love to you last Christmas Eve, but I'm tired of apologizing for it, sick of beating myself up about it. How can I apologize when it felt so damn good... so damn right?"

And suddenly his mouth was covering hers, warm, firm and once again, Faith was lost in the sensual storm that was Ryan.

Chapter Four

No one kissed like he did, Faith thought dazedly. His mouth felt like it was made to fit hers. He plucked at her with movements that struck her as languorous and demanding at once; he sandwiched her lower lip between his and bit at the sensitive flesh lightly, making her gasp. When she opened her mouth, he slid his tongue between her lips, a sleek, sensual invader. Ripples of pleasu re cascaded down her spine.

He made a sound of male gratification as he tasted her, sweeping his tongue everywhere, exploring her…possessing her. Faith responded in the only way her muddled brain and buzzing body seemed to know how to respond to Ryan's sensual assaults—wholeheartedly. She tangled her tongue with his, absorbing his flavor, feeling their kiss in the very core of her being. She'd noticed that pregnancy had made her body extra sensitive, her sense of smell and taste more acute, her breasts plagued by a dull, not unpleasant ache.

Adding Ryan to the formula only seemed to amp up her sensitivities to a whole new level of feeling.

She tightened her hold on his hard shoulders, pulling herself toward him, pressing their upper bodies together. Feeling her breasts press against the solidness of his chest made her moan softly into his mouth. As if electrified by the sound, Ryan leaned into her further. His hands moved along the side of her body, molding his palms over her rib cage as if he wanted to feel her heartbeat. He touched the sides of her breasts and gave a low, tense moan, deepening their kiss. Pleasure rippled through her, the strength of it shocking her. Even through her coat and clothing, his caress had the power to make her forget her inhibitions and recall her elemental femininity all too well.

A shock went through his body. They broke apart. He cursed a second later when his thigh hit the gearshift.

"Are you all right?" Faith asked anxiously.

"Yeah. This just isn't an ideal location for this," he muttered, trying to arrange his long body in the seat. What *this* actually meant penetrated Faith's lust-befuddled consciousness.

"It's not the ideal *situation* for it, either," she said starkly, leaning back, breaking their contact. She stared out the front window, letting her arms fall to her sides, regretting the loss of Ryan's hard male body almost as much as she did the feeling of his hands sliding off her torso. She breathed deeply, trying to find some sanity. One second they'd been pressed together too tight to slip a match between them, and the next, they were separate...

...alone.

She suffered through a tense moment of silence before he spoke.

"Just because the situation is unusual doesn't mean it's wrong."

She couldn't help but give a bark of hysterical laughter. "*Unusual?* Don't you think you're stating it a bit mildly? I'm pregnant with my dead husband's friend's baby, whom

I hardly know. I'd say that's a bit more than unusual. Ryan? What are you doing?" she asked in amazement when he unfastened his seat belt and reached for the door handle.

"I'm walking you to the front door. We'll talk about this more tomorrow."

"Tomorrow?" she asked, eyes wide.

"Yeah," he said, pulling the latch. He glanced back at her. She saw that his features were tight with regret. "I didn't mean to upset you. I don't know how many times I can say that without sounding like a fool or a liar."

Faith shut her eyelids and took a deep breath to restore her calm. "I'm okay, Ryan. I'm not upset." She opened her eyes and regarded him. "You have to admit, though... this whole thing is awfully strange."

"Strange, maybe," he conceded, swinging his long legs onto the driveway. "Not awful, though. Far from awful."

Later that night Faith lay in bed wide awake, her hand curved protectively over her belly, staring blankly at the ceiling. What was she going to do about Ryan's decision to move to the area? Did she have a right to do or say anything? Didn't he have a right to be near his own child, if he chose?

What was she going to do about him *period*?

Despite her anxious thoughts, her errant brain kept returning to that kiss in the car. She'd learned at Christmas that logic and kissing Ryan did not go hand in hand. For the past three months thoughts of that night would sneak up to plague her during the dark, quiet hours when she had nothing else to distract her from them. In the interim of Ryan's absence she'd almost convinced herself that what had happened on that night was an aberration of memory. Surely Ryan's kiss couldn't be that wonderful, his touch that powerful.

But now he'd kissed her again, and she could no longer deny the truth.

The first part of that visit on Christmas Eve had gone reasonably well, Faith recalled. At first she'd been aware of a certain tension in the air upon seeing Ryan so unexpectedly for the first time in two years. He hadn't been given a leave of absence to attend Jesse's funeral, so she hadn't seen him then. Every time she'd met with him before, it'd been within the safety of a large gathering...within the security of her marriage.

Faith hadn't fully realized until later that evening, however, that the thick tension between them on Christmas Eve had been of the sexual variety.

Perhaps she shouldn't have served him a glass of her spiked Christmas punch? It'd be convenient to blame what happened later that night on alcohol consumption, but Faith suspected very strongly that Ryan had been right when he'd said the experience felt unstoppable, Christmas punch or no.

She vividly recalled how stunned and pleased she'd been when he'd called that night and said he was nearby.

"This is wonderful," Faith said when he entered the house, bringing a brief blast of cold winter air with him. "What are you doing back in Michigan?"

"I'm visiting my sister, Mari," Ryan said, his gaze dropping over her robe-covered figure regretfully. "I'm sorry it's so late. I should come back tomorrow."

"Don't be ridiculous! Come with me to the kitchen. I have some punch left over. I'll get us a cup and we'll talk."

"*Jesse used to say your punch had more juice than an F-15.*"

"*The way he used to drink it, he was right,*" she said, smiling as she glanced back at him.

He chuckled. "*I don't want to be any bother. I'll stop by another time...if that's all right,*" he added cautiously.

"*Of course it's all right, but you're not a bother now. I was only going to bed because I didn't have anything better to do.*"

"*Were you here alone?*" he asked when she flipped on the kitchen light. She did a double take when she saw the concerned expression on his face.

"*I wasn't alone. I went over to a friend's house—she's my office manager, actually.*"

"*Oh, yeah. Jane, right?*"

She paused, stunned. "*How do you know about Jane?*"

He shrugged. "*Jesse used to read me your letters.*"

She blushed and glanced away.

"*Not...not all of them, just portions,*" he hurried to say. "*I hope you don't mind. Entertainment on a deployment is kind of scarce, but warmth and affection from a loved one is an even rarer commodity.*"

"So you shared some of Jesse's?" she murmured.

"Not in a weird way or anything," he said, looking a little uncomfortable.

She laughed softly. "Don't worry, I don't take offense. There was nothing in my letters that couldn't have been read on the base announcement system, anyway. I just tend to ramble on in my letters like a crazy woman."

"I liked them. You're a good writer. You could get published, telling all those stories about your practice. Some of them were really funny. I could sense your personality through your words."

"Thanks," she said, both flustered and flattered.

"So...you were with Jane tonight?"

"Yes," she said, swinging open the refrigerator. "She has a huge family. Half the people there assumed I was a long lost cousin. It was nice," she said, pulling out the plastic-covered large bowl she'd used to transport the punch.

"Really?" he asked pointedly.

"What do you mean?" she asked, twisting her chin to look over her shoulder.

"I was at a family gathering tonight, where I

was the outsider," he admitted, stepping closer and closing the refrigerator door for her. "I was at my sister's in-laws' family gathering in Harbor Town. I'm glad you felt like you belonged. Personally, I felt the urge to run a couple times, but I was there at my sister's request."

She paused in the action of removing two cups from the cabinet. "Well...maybe I did exaggerate my comfort level with Jane's family a little bit. Still, it's nice not to be alone. On Christmas."

"Yeah. Now we can not be alone together," he said, smiling.

Their gazes stuck. She realized she'd frozen in her task. She hurried to fill their glasses.

Ryan's eyebrows shot up a moment later when he took a drink.

"Jesse wasn't exaggerating. Now I get why they call it punch," he said, blinking.

She laughed. "We'll keep it to one glass, but we could use some Christmas cheer, right?"

"Right."

She smiled and turned and replaced the bowl in the refrigerator.

"Merry Christmas," she said when she rejoined Ryan a moment later, holding up her glass.

"Merry Christmas." They watched each other over the rims of their glasses as they drank.

"I'm sure you have plans for Christmas," she said after they talked a while. "But I hope you'll consider yourself invited here, if you have any free time. I'll make a nice lunch or dinner for us. And your sister and her family are invited, too, if they'd like to come."

"That's very generous," he said slowly. "I guess I shouldn't be surprised."

"What do you mean?" she asked.

"Jesse used to say you didn't know a stranger."

"You're not a stranger," she said, smiling. "I feel like I know you as well as some people that I see every day of my life." The full awareness of what she'd just said—of how much she'd meant it—seemed to soak into her brain slowly. When it fully penetrated, she'd looked at Ryan cautiously, her breath stuck in her lungs.

He stared at her. Black lashes emphasized eyes that were so dark brown they verged on black. She would have thought eyes that color *would be cold in appearance, but Ryan's shone with warmth.*

With heat?

She spilled a little of her punch on her robe when she stood too abruptly. Ryan sprung up almost as rapidly. She laughed awkwardly as she wiped away the red liquid with her hand.

"Clumsy," she muttered under her breath. Now her hand was all sticky. "Uh, excuse me... I just need to..."

"Faith?" he called when she rushed over to the kitchen sink and turned on the water.

"Yes?" she asked, glancing around to see he'd followed her and set his half-empty glass on the counter.

"You don't feel like a stranger to me, either."

She stared, her mouth partially opened in amazement at his stark declaration.

His deep voice seemed to ring in her head three months later as she lay in bed. Faith kept telling herself to stop remembering—reliving—every detail of that night. She told herself to forget.

The problem was, part of her rebelled against that very idea. Part of her clung on to the memories of feeling so alive...so cherished. He'd made her feel so special, made her so aware of her femininity, made her prize again what Jesse had found replaceable.

Part of her treasured the memories of Ryan, and that part was only growing since he'd come back into her life. That realization worried Faith.

It worried her a lot.

She was in the process of doing Saturday morning chores when she heard a car door slam. Her heart lurched against her breastbone when she peeked out the window and saw Ryan's car in the driveway. He'd said that he'd stop by again today, but she hadn't expected him so early.

She dropped the curtain and glanced at herself in the vanity mirror. She'd washed her hair this morning, but hadn't styled it. It'd dried into a wild riot of curls, which she'd restrained in a low ponytail at her neck. She wore an old pair of low-rise jeans and a simple white T-shirt. The shirt was a lot tighter than she ever remembered it being before, and the jeans kept slipping down her hips while she worked, resulting in her newly expanding belly protruding over the waistband.

A brisk knock resounded down the hallway. Topsy charged to the front door, yipping ferociously the entire time. Panicked, Faith flung open her closet and grabbed an old flannel shirt. She hurriedly slipped it on, and then hitched up her uncooperative jeans. She grabbed Topsy before she opened the front door.

Ryan stood there in the sunshine holding a toolbox. His dark hair fluttered in the spring breeze. He wore a pair of well-fitted jeans, brown work boots and a dark blue thermal shirt with a T-shirt beneath it. He pretty much epitomized the sexy tool man that every female with a healthy pulse on the planet would love to invite into her house.

She mentally rolled her eyes at the errant, ridiculous thought and opened the screen door for him.

"Is this a good time?" Ryan asked.

"Er...a good time for what?" she wondered, her gaze running over the line of his slightly whiskered jaw and well-shaped mouth.

His lips tilted ever so slightly.

"To fix your back door. Unless you had something else in mind. I'm flexible."

Faith realized his gaze had dropped. She'd

tried to close the flannel shirt over the revealing T-shirt, but Topsy had wiggled her way into the opening, parting the material. Her nipples prickled beneath Ryan's warm glance. Heat rushed into her cheeks.

"Fixing the back door would be great. If you're sure you don't mind?" she asked, flustered. She tried to tug the flannel shirt closed over the strip of bare skin above her jeans. She backed up so that he could enter. If he were just a few inches taller, he'd have to duck his head to not hit the doorframe. As soon as the door was closed, she set down Topsy, who yipped and frolicked on Ryan's boots and around his ankles. The puppy wagged her entire bottom, not just her tail, as he bent to pet her.

"Am I interrupting anything?" Ryan asked after he'd stood.

"No," she said, leading him to the kitchen, hurriedly buttoning the flannel shirt. "I was just doing some cleaning, and I have to attack the den later."

"Attack?" he asked. She heard the smile in his voice before she glanced back to see it. His wind-ruffled dark hair fell attractively on his forehead. "Sounds pretty hardcore."

"I keep procrastinating on it," Faith said as she watched him set down his toolbox next to the back door. She realized she was staring at his rear end as he bent over and glanced away, blushing.

"What's the hurry?" Ryan asked, flipping open the lid on the metal box.

"Well, the baby coming, I guess."

He paused at that, his head swinging around. She felt herself being examined by his incisive stare.

She gave him a weak smile. "The den is going to be the nursery. I have to clear it all out before I can start to decorate and buy the furniture."

She saw the color wash out of his face beneath his tan. He just stood there, holding a hammer and looking stunned.

"Ryan? Are you okay?"

After a second he nodded. He stepped toward the door. "It's really going to happen, isn't it?" he said after a moment. "You're actually going to have a baby."

She nodded, giving him a quizzical glance. He shook his head slightly, as if to clear it. "I woke up this morning, wondering if it had all been a dream," she heard him mutter as he lifted the claw of the hammer to loosen the piece of plywood.

"Like I said, it takes a while to set in. It seems a little surreal to me all over again, with you being here," she admitted.

For a stretched second they looked at one another. Then Ryan inhaled and returned to his task. "I'll come and help you with the den after I finish here. Do me a favor?"

"What?" Faith asked.

"Don't lift anything heavy or overexert yourself."

She crossed her arms at her waist. "You make it sound like pregnancy is a frailty. I'm very healthy."

He arched his eyebrows at her defiance, his mouth twitching in a grin. "I agree. I'd just like to keep it that way."

She couldn't help returning his small smile. It was difficult to get miffed at him when he was so charming. Still, she wouldn't want to set a precedent with him for allowing heavy-handedness.

"I'm perfectly capable of taking care of myself. And the baby," she said, quietly but firmly.

"There's no doubt about that. But I'm the

baby's father, and I want to help. No reason for me not to do the heavy jobs," he said, pulling on the hammer and prying the nails out of her back door like it was made of butter instead of wood. He gave her a sideways glance. "*I'm* capable, too, Faith. And willing."

Faith couldn't argue with that. He was, indeed, capable…at many things. She wasn't sure how to respond to that knowing look in his eyes when he'd admitted to being *willing*, as well. She felt her cheeks heating and figured it was best to retreat for now.

"Would you like me to make you some coffee?"

He shook his head, his attention now so entirely on his task she might have imagined the heat in his eyes right now. "I'm good."

"Then I'll be in the den."

"I'll be there in a while," Ryan replied briskly.

True to his word, he joined her in the den a little less than an hour later. Faith glanced up when he entered the room and towered over where she sat on the floor next to her old hope chest.

"All finished in the kitchen," he said, glancing around the room. His gaze stuck on an old Holland High School booster banner tacked on the bulletin board. "I thought you said this was the den. It looks like your old bedroom."

"It was," Faith admitted. "When I bought the house from Mom and Dad, it sort of became a combination den and storage room. I have another guest bedroom for visitors, and I moved into the master suite. This room gets the best morning sunlight, though, so I thought it'd be ideal for the nursery."

She held up the high school report card she'd found in the trunk. "I can't believe my mother saved some of this junk," she said before she started to throw the card into a plastic garbage bag. Ryan halted her with a hand at her wrist. She glanced up in surprise when he took the report card from her. He stood there, examining it, an amused expression lighting his carved features.

"Straight A's in trigonometry, chemistry, AP English and economics." His eyebrows went up. "A C minus in gym class?"

Faith blinked in embarrassment and stretched to snatch the card out of his hand. She tossed it into the garbage bag and gave him a rueful glance.

"We had softball that quarter. I can't hit a ball for anything. Let's hope the baby gets your athletic abilities and reflexes, and not mine," she mumbled, smiling grudgingly. She looked up in amazement at the sound of his deep laughter. He knelt on the carpet next to her, still chuckling. Her grin widened. She went still when he leaned toward her and picked up a curl that had fallen over her shoulder. She didn't move as he rubbed the coil of hair between his fingers, his expression growing thoughtful.

"I hope the baby gets your curls." He met her stare. "And your smile."

She stared at him, wide-eyed. Suddenly, the space between them seemed very small. The air itself seemed to grow heavy, like a pocket had just been formed around them and was shrinking by the second. She couldn't think of what to say.

She couldn't think, period.

"Can I ask you a favor?" he asked in a subdued, serious tone.

She just nodded, her lips falling open. He met her gaze solemnly.

"Can I touch our baby?"

Chapter Five

When she didn't speak immediately, she saw his muscular throat tighten as he swallowed. "It's just that it's been really hard for me to absorb this. It might help me. It might make it more real somehow..."

He trailed off when she just continued to stare at him. He tightened his hands on his thighs.

"Never mind," he said gruffly. "I'm sorry I mentioned it."

"No," Faith said quickly, regret filtering through her entrancement. His request was incredibly intimate, but not in the sexual sense. It was as if her brain didn't quite know how to interpret his question. "I'm sorry. You just took me by surprise," she said, coming up on her knees and facing him. She smiled nervously. "I understand about finding it hard to accept. I didn't really start to soak it in until I saw the ultrasound."

"What was it like?"

"Incredible. You could see the heart beating," she said in a hushed voice.

"Wow." A strained silence followed as they just looked at each other. "Do you think I could come? For the next ultrasound?"

She nodded.

"Thanks."

"I have a picture of the baby, Ryan. I'll show it to you."

"That'd be great."

She told herself to stand and get the ultrasound photo, but instead she remained kneeling there. Her heart went out to him. How difficult it must be for him. She had the baby with her every second of every day—a warm, wonderful secret growing within her very flesh. It seemed so unfair, to keep him separate from that awesome experience.

Slowly she began to unbutton the flannel

shirt. He went utterly still, the only exception being his dark-eyed gaze flickering downward, following the path of her fingers.

Faith hesitated when she saw that the thin T-shirt had again wormed its way up over the nearly insubstantial bump in her belly, while her low-riding jeans had gone in the opposite direction. She willfully ignored the heat that rushed into her cheeks, however. Hadn't Ryan just asked if he could come to the next ultrasound? She might as well get used to allowing him to see her naked stomach.

She opened the flaps of the flannel shirt and glanced up with effort. Her hands trembled slightly as she held the fabric when she saw that his dark eyes weren't trained on her belly, but on her breasts pressing tightly against the white cotton. The silence seemed to take on weight. His gaze lingered, and then lowered over her.

Had she just thought that his request was intimate, but not sexual? She'd been wrong, Faith realized as her heartbeat began to throb in her ears and he stared at her belly. It was both.

In spades.

Her mouth went dry when he reached with

one hand, and gently pulled up the T-shirt to her waist. She held her breath until it burned in her lungs when he placed his hand over her abdomen. She knew from experience that her belly felt taut and smooth. His hand looked dark next to her pale skin, his fingers long and strong. He nearly encompassed her width. A warm pressure spread at her core, making her ache.

She glanced up at him, her curiosity overcoming her embarrassment. His face looked rapt. When his gaze flickered upward, she gave him a shaky smile.

"Pretty awesome, huh?" she said softly.

"Amazing," he agreed, looking like he meant it in the literal, not everyday usage of the word. He moved his hand. His palm was warm against her bare skin.

"Can you feel the baby moving yet?" he asked.

She shook her head. In his leaned-over position, his face was very close to hers. She could smell his spicy, clean scent. They'd taken to talking in hushed tones, as if they were conversing at a sacred event. Which they were, Faith supposed.

"The doctor says I should at around sixteen

to twenty-two weeks. Maybe later, since it's my first pregnancy."

"So this *is* your first pregnancy."

She blinked in surprise, but then caught what he'd meant. It was possible that she'd gotten pregnant before, and lost the baby. "Yes. I've never been pregnant until now. Jesse wasn't interested in having children," she said gently.

He didn't say anything, just glanced back down to his hand on her stomach. He moved it slightly, spiking tendrils of pleasure through her flesh.

"Ryan?" she asked quietly. He looked up at her, his expression solemn.

"Did you? Want a child? Someday, I mean?" she clarified.

"Yes."

She gave a tremulous smile. The conviction in his voice had been absolute.

"Well…even if the timing and circumstances weren't what you might have wanted, I'm glad that your wish came true," she whispered.

"Thank you. For making it come true," he said quietly.

Her lips parted, but she couldn't speak. She

was caught in his stare. Neither of them spoke when he lifted his hand. Somehow she knew what he was about to do. She didn't protest when he gently cupped her right breast. The heavy, pleasurable ache at her center amplified to a slow burn.

"You're changing here, too," he said gruffly.

She stifled a gasp when his fingers moved, ever so slightly, grazing a sensitive nipple. "Yes."

"Are you planning on breast-feeding?" he asked.

When she didn't immediately respond, his gaze flashed up to her face. She nodded, her throat too tight with emotion to speak. His nostrils flared. He seemed to come to himself. He dropped his hand and stood. Faith looked up at him helplessly. His face was rigid and difficult to read, but his tense muscles and hard body betrayed his arousal.

He excused himself and walked out of the room, leaving her spinning in confusion and desire.

After taking a few minutes to compose himself, Ryan returned to the den. Regret hit him when he saw Faith glance up at him from where she still sat on the floor, her face looking pale, her eyes huge. She'd rebuttoned the flannel shirt, which amplified his guilt, but also gladdened him. All in all, he thought it was best for the time being that she cover herself from his greedy gaze. The last thing he wanted to do was to alienate her, but seeing the subtle transformation of her lovely body had moved him deeply.

It had also been one of the most erotic experiences he could ever imagine—touching her. If that had been true on Christmas Eve, it was even more so now that his child grew inside of her.

A child.

Their baby.

And people said miracles didn't happen anymore. Couldn't they see they occurred every day, right in front of their eyes?

"What should I tackle first?" he asked, forcing his mind to the mundane and glancing around the room. He was glad to see the tension seep out of her face.

"Oh, well I suppose you could start with the closet? Pretty much everything in there is stuff that I've already gone through and want to throw away."

"What about all this furniture?" he asked, inspecting the large cherry desk, bureau and full-size bed.

"I was planning on hiring movers to do that. I'm going to donate the bed and bureau to the Salvation Army. They said they'd come and pick it up with their truck if I got the items out into the driveway. As for the desk, I'm moving that to the guest bedroom," she said, standing.

Ryan nodded, assessing the items. "I can do it today. I'll run into town and rent a hand truck, then stop by the Salvation Army and ask them to pick up the bed and bureau later this afternoon." He noticed Faith's amazed expression. "But if you'd rather I worked on the closet instead, that's fine, too."

"No, I just hadn't expected that it all could be taken care of so quickly by one person. Are you sure? It seems like such a big job."

"Not if I have the right tools to do it with," Ryan said. He caught her gaze and gave her a smile. He hoped she recognized it as an apology for pawing her earlier. Not that he'd considered it pawing, by any means. More like carnal worship, but he couldn't really tell

Faith that without making more of a fool of himself than he already had.

"I'll be back in less than an hour. How about if I bring us back some lunch, too?"

"That'd be great." She gave him a shaky smile, and he thought he might have been forgiven.

He hoped so, anyway.

When he returned with the rented hand truck, he taped all the drawers together on the desk and moved it into the spare bedroom. Afterward, they took a break. He got everything ready for their lunch while Faith admired her newly fixed back door, complete with not just one, but two sturdy-looking brass locks. She opened it and gazed at the back yard. Topsy was almost immediately there, panting to get outside. Faith laughed and let the puppy run into the yard.

"This is great. I used to have to take her out the front and go around the house to let her into the fenced-in area. Thank you for fixing it, Ryan," she said, coming toward him and accepting the sandwich and salad he offered her, along with a carton of skim milk.

"My pleasure," Ryan said, watching Topsy

through the window over the sink. She zipped from place to place, sniffing every bush and new bloom avidly. He laughed. Faith looked over and smiled. She really liked his deep, booming laugh. "She's like a hyperactive bee out there sniffing those bushes," he said.

"I didn't call her Topsy-Turvy for nothing," Faith said wryly, setting out napkins and forks for them. "Are you a mind reader?" she asked a few seconds later as she sat at the breakfast nook and unwrapped her sandwich. "This is my favorite from the City Deli," she said, grinning and picking up the vegetarian sandwich. "How did you know?"

"I just asked the lady behind the counter if she knew you and what you liked. She did, apparently," he said, watching her as she took a healthy bite.

"That's Celia," Faith said after she'd swallowed. "One of the many advantages of living in a small town. The townsfolk know all your habits and secrets, both bad and good. I'll bet Celia was very interested in getting you whatever you wanted," she said with wry amusement before she took another bite. Celia was a kind, attractive woman in her late thirties who had never made a secret about her open admiration for the male of the species. Since Ryan was a prime example of that, she knew for a fact he'd been the target of Celia's earthy flirtation. Jesse had certainly seemed to be the object of it whenever he came to Holland. Jesse had soaked up Celia's attentions, Faith recalled.

"I think Celia was more interested in the fact that I wanted to know exactly what *you* wanted," Ryan said after he'd swallowed his first bite of his roast beef and Swiss.

Faith gave him a surprised glance. She had to hand it to him. That was the perfect response to silence her vague uneasiness.

As if she had a right to get miffed at the thought of him flirting with another woman, she thought, mentally rolling her eyes at herself. Jesse had really done a number on her, for her to get this paranoid.

She forked her salad slowly, steeling herself for bringing up a potentially dicey topic when she and Ryan were getting along so well together.

"Did you give any more thought about what you said last night…about moving to Michigan, I mean?"

He nodded as he chewed, waiting until

he swallowed. He took a swig of ice water. "Yeah, I did. I called my sister, Mari, late last night and had a conversation with her about it."

Faith set down her fork, shocked. This was not the response she'd expected. She'd thought maybe he'd had time to reconsider his impulsive decision to relocate his home and business—his entire life. "You had a conversation with her about moving to Michigan?"

"Yes, and about the baby." Her mouth fell open in amazement. "I hope that's okay. Mari and I are really close. And like you said earlier, it's really big news. Talking to her helped me get my bearings a little bit. Faith?" he asked, his dark eyebrows pinching together as he looked at her. "Is that okay?"

She blinked. "Yes. Of course. Like I said, I'll be telling my parents soon. And Jane knows already. Of course you wanted to tell your sister." She picked up her fork again. "How did Mari take it?"

"She was floored."

"Naturally," Faith muttered, suddenly feeling nervous for some reason. Was she worried about what Mari would think of her? Would

Ryan's sister perhaps disapprove of the unusual circumstances?

Ryan gave her a warm glance. "But then she really started to get excited." He seemed to hesitate for a second, and then took a bite out of his sandwich.

"Ryan, what is it?" Faith asked, sensing he was holding back. He took several seconds to respond.

"It's just… Mari wants to come to Michigan to visit tomorrow." He gave her a fleeting glance, and Faith realized he seemed uncomfortable. "She…um…wants to meet you."

"Oh."

He set down his sandwich. "You don't have to, if you don't want to."

"I do want to," Faith said breathlessly. "It's just…"

"What?"

"It all seems so…*serious*."

They just looked at each other for a moment.

"Having a baby is serious, though. Isn't it?" Ryan finally said slowly.

"Yeah," Faith admitted. She gave Ryan a helpless sort of glance, and for some reason, the weightiness inherent to their conversation—their entire situation—temporarily lifted. Simultaneously Ryan grinned and Faith burst into hysterical laughter.

"I'm sorry," Faith said a moment later, wiping a few tears caused by her laughing jag off her cheek with a paper napkin. "This situation is so strange. I hope your sister doesn't think I'm an...*oddity.*"

"She'll think you're exactly what you are. She'll think you're wonderful," Ryan said simply. Her laughter faded when he touched her hand where it sat on the table, ever so briefly. Nerves all along the skin of her hand and forearm flickered to life.

After her heartbeat went back to normal following that caress, they managed to have a nice lunch together. Ryan's easy conversation about practical matters settled her unrest about his sudden presence in her life, and her confusion about how she was supposed to feel about it. After they'd eaten and cleaned up, Ryan resumed his furniture-moving project, and Faith hauled sacks filled with garbage out of the room. It fascinated her to watch him work, to observe how methodical and efficient he was in breaking down the bed into easily movable pieces, strapping the bureau drawers closed with duct tape, then maneuvering the large pieces of furniture through the door while he held them vertical on the metal truck.

In what seemed like no time, the furniture was neatly piled at the end of her driveway. Before she knew it, the Salvation Army truck had come to retrieve it, and a project she'd dreaded undertaking was done within a matter of hours.

"You're a miracle of efficiency," she told him as they both watched through the window as the two workers from the Salvation Army got into the truck and drove away. She turned and gazed at the nursery-to-be. Now that the room was empty, the possibilities of transforming it into a wonderful place for the baby filled her with excitement. She clapped her hands together eagerly and gave Ryan an irrepressible grin.

"Thank you so much."

"You're welcome," he said, his warm gaze running over her face.

"Do you want to know how I plan to decorate?" she asked, suddenly feeling like a kid with a secret she longed to share.

"Of course."

She swept across the room and gestured over the entire north wall. "I plan to paint a mural here—bright, eye-catching colors, and the cradle will go here, and a set of drawers here, and a baby changing table here," she explained as she moved around the room. "I'd like to hire someone to come in and do some built-in shelves on this wall—something that'll last, that can be used even when the baby is in high school. Now that you've cleaned out the room for me, I can order a new carpet. I haven't decided what color to do the walls in. It'll depend on whether or not I decide to know the sex during the next ultrasound." She turned toward him and paused. "I mean, what *we* decide," she added weakly.

"Sounds like you have big plans," he said, inspecting the blank wall as if he saw something there she didn't. "I'll pay for half of the redecoration."

"Oh… I didn't mean…well, I suppose that'd be okay," she fumbled. He'd said it so unexpectedly, she hadn't had time to prepare. He was the baby's father. It was a perfectly reasonable offer.

"Can I build the shelves?"

"*Can* you do something like that?" Faith asked, eyes wide.

Ryan's nod was entirely confident. "My father taught me carpentry. We used to take on projects together as a hobby when I was a kid. I did the built-in bookshelves in my condominium in San Francisco. Here," he paused, digging in his jean pocket and extracting his cell phone. He tapped a few buttons and handed the device to her. "It doesn't have to look exactly like that. I can design it for whatever you want and need for the baby."

"Oh, it's amazing," Faith exclaimed, staring at a photo of beautifully crafted floor to ceiling maple shelves and cabinets. She glanced at Ryan with amazement. "I can't believe you built that. Jesse used to say you were the best pilot he'd ever met," she said quietly. "He said your reaction times were off the charts. And here you could have had a career as a carpenter, as well."

"Not likely," Ryan said, grinning and putting away his phone.

"Yeah, I guess you don't get the adrenaline rush with carpentry that you do with flying." For some reason a jolt of disappointment and irritation had gone through her when she saw his appealing, but undoubtedly cocky, smile. She was all too familiar with the rootless flyboy type. A man like Ryan would never be satisfied with a career like carpentry, or *anything* that kept him so grounded.

"My love of flying was never about the adrenaline rush. Or at least not primarily about that."

"Really?" Faith asked, her eyebrows quirked upward and a small, slightly incredulous smile on her face. She started to walk away, but blinked in surprise when Ryan caught her hand and pulled slightly until she swung to face him.

"Really," he said emphatically, an odd expression shadowing his visage. His gaze narrowed on her. "Why are you so convinced that I'm an adrenaline junkie, hell-raising pilot?"

"Come on, Ryan," she said with soft remonstrance. "I was a military wife. Do you think I don't know the personalities of the majority of Air Force pilots? I know it's a stereotype, but a pretty well-earned one, at least in my opinion…"

She trailed off, knowing she'd made a mistake when she saw the fire flash in his eyes.

"So that's what I'm up against?" he asked, his voice quiet, but commanding. "Not just Jesse's bad behaviors, but your stereotype about all pilots being jacked-up jerks always looking for the next high over the horizon, be it with a hot, fast jet or a hot, fast woman. Is that it, Faith?"

She blushed at his graphic description, but bristled at it, as well. "I'm not going to apologize for my experience."

"Fine," he replied quickly, pulling her a little closer until the lapels of their shirts brushed together. This close, she could see the inky black color of his lashes and the gleam of the lamplight in his ebony eyes. "Just do me the favor of not judging me by it until you've had a chance to broaden your horizons."

"I suppose you think I need more of the experience that I had with you on Christmas Eve?" she said sarcastically, and immediately regretted it. His nostrils flared at her challenge. His head lowered until their mouths were only inches apart. Against her will, Faith felt herself close the distance between them infinitesimally.

"That wasn't what I was talking about,"

he said quietly, his gaze roaming over her face and landing on her lips. "But honestly? Yeah, I think that's precisely the kind of experience you need. With *me*," he added succinctly, causing the burn in her cheeks to transfer to other parts of her body.

"I'm not about to make that kind of mistake anytime soon," she whispered shakily. She went still when he suddenly palmed her jaw and spoke so close to her mouth that she felt his warm breath fanning her lips.

"I'll be ready for you whenever you change your mind."

Faith blinked, disoriented, when he dropped his hand and walked away.

Ryan stalked to the kitchen, anger and arousal surging in equal measure through his veins. By the time he'd gathered all his tools, closed his toolbox and retrieved the rented metal truck, regret had joined the potent brew.

He should feel more compassionate toward Faith, given everything she'd been through with Jesse's faithless ways. He'd never been more infuriated at Jesse for what his friend had done, wounding such a lovely, generous woman.

What if Faith could never trust a man again? The possibility was too terrible to consider for long. Somehow he had to convince her that this strong, powerful attraction they shared for one another wasn't the sign of a lustful fling, but the stable basis for something real...something lasting.

He paused in the hallway next to the living room when he saw her approaching. His heart sank when he saw her expression.

"Ryan, I'm sorry—"

"No," he cut her off more abruptly than he'd intended and took a deep breath, briefly shutting his eyes. He opened them again, pinning her with his stare. "*I'm* sorry."

She gave him a shaky smile. He hated seeing the uncertainty in her green eyes. She waved at the metal truck. "Thank you again. I can't believe all you accomplished today."

"All *we* accomplished."

She nodded.

"I'll give you a call tomorrow morning and let you know about getting together with Mari? If you still want to, that is."

"I do want to," she said.

He gave her a small smile, appreciating her attempt to make things right between them again. All in all, he thought it was best that he get out of there before he said another stupid thing…or worse, touched her again. It was becoming increasingly hard to walk away after he felt her warm, soft skin beneath his fingertips, saw the way her lips parted as if in anticipation of his kiss—

He realized he was staring at her mouth again and charged toward the front door.

"I'll call you tomorrow, then."

"Okay," he heard her say in a small voice from behind him.

Fifteen minutes later he dropped the key to his hotel room on the night table and stalked toward the bathroom, where he turned on the shower.

A good dousing in cold water helped, but it couldn't extinguish the sound of Faith's voice ringing in his head like a sexy taunt.

He toweled off and shrugged on a pair of briefs and jeans, not bothering to button them all the way. He sat on the bed and grabbed the remote control. The baseball game on TV didn't distract him from hearing Faith's voice much better than the cold shower had.

I suppose you think I need more of the

experience that I had with you on Christmas Eve?

Hell, *yes* that's what he thought. What sane male in existence wouldn't think about repeating such a phenomenal experience, almost to the exclusion of everything else?

Even though he'd ritualistically forced himself not to dwell on what had happened between them on Christmas Eve, his powers were running thin now that he'd seen Faith again. Now that he'd touched her.

Now that he'd witnessed firsthand the miraculous result of making love to her that night.

Christmas Eve.
He remembered Faith's radiant smile as they'd sat there together in the breakfast nook, sipping their Christmas punch. How could a woman possibly be so sweet and sexy as hell all at once?

"You're not a stranger," Faith said, beaming at him. *"I feel like I know you as well as some people that I see every day of my life."*
She faltered, as if suddenly second-guessing what she'd just said. Did she realize how

uninhibited, how generous...how appealing *she'd sounded? She glanced away, her expression frozen. He saw her pulse thrumming delicately at her throat above the modest nightgown she wore with a white robe tied securely over it. As he watched, her heartbeat leaped.*

She peeked over at him cautiously through a fall of dark, glorious waves and curls. Her cheeks and lips were flushed a becoming pink. He wondered if it was wishful thinking on his part, but her green eyes looked glazed with desire.

She spilled punch on her robe when she stood too abruptly. Ryan sprang up almost as rapidly. She laughed awkwardly as she wiped her hand over the upper swell of a soft-looking, firm breast, trying to dry the red fluid.

"Clumsy. Uh, excuse me... I just need to..."

He followed her, drawn to her like a bee to honey. "Faith?" he called when she rushed over to the kitchen sink and turned on the water.

"Yes?" she asked, glancing around, her eyes huge in her face.

"You don't feel like a stranger to me, either."

The words had just popped out of his mouth. This entire interaction with Faith had taken on a charged tone. Something about it felt alarmingly imperative, as if he'd been planning it in some part of his brain he kept secret even from himself for a long time now... waiting for it for most of his life.

When he realized the bizarre direction of his thoughts, he blinked and stepped back. He was not typically a whimsical man.

He was never a whimsical man.

"I should go. It's late."

Her eyes widened. "Oh, don't rush off," she said regretfully as she wiped off her hands. "I don't know what's wrong with me. I'm not usually so jumpy—"

He shoved his hands in his jean pockets and gave a polite nod, looking away willfully when he noticed how pretty she was in her discomposure. "I'll just go get my coat."

Something had caught his eye as he'd tried to make a hasty exit. He paused, despite his better judgment, and then slowly walked to a bookcase in Faith's living room. He picked up one of the photos on her bookshelves.

"That was taken at Bagram Airfield, I

think," Faith said from behind him, refer-
ring to the picture Ryan held.

He set down the photograph of Jesse and
him wearing flight suits and standing in front
of the brand-new Raptor they'd just test pi-
loted. As usual, Jesse looked unabashedly,
boyishly happy, as if he couldn't think of a
place he'd rather be in the world than in a
blistering desert seven thousand miles from
his wife.

"Yeah," Ryan said, turning to face her. The
air seemed to hum with an electrical charge.
Thus far on his unexpected visit, they hadn't
broached the topic of Jesse or his death. Jesse
and four other airmen had been on a search
and rescue mission for a fellow pilot who had
been forced to eject from his plane. Four of
the search team had been killed in an accidental helicopter crash in the Kunar province
in Afghanistan, including Jesse. Only the helicopter pilot had survived. Ryan's wing had
been hit hard by the loss of five of their own.

The pilot that had survived had, ironically,
been Jesse's girlfriend, Melanie Shane.

Faith's smile looked a little sad. "Jesse always spoke very fondly of you. It was obvious how much he respected you."

"He was a good friend," he said, searching her face for some sign of what she thought of her dead husband.

"He'll have been gone for a year in January," she said suddenly, studying the carpet.

An awkward silence ensued.

"I'm so sorry you lost such a—"

"I can't tell you how sorry I am for your—"

Both of them stopped midsentence when they realized the other spoke a similar sentiment. Ryan winced slightly.

"You shouldn't sympathize with me. Jesse was your husband. That's the cruelest loss of all."

Faith swallowed convulsively. He wished he could read her expression. "In many ways, the people you serve with are closer than family," she said quietly. "You spent time with Jesse, day in and day out. You depended on each other. I know how much he admired you. Of course you'd feel his loss deeply," she said, her gaze traveling over his face.

"Are you still struggling, Faith? With his loss?" Ryan asked, both curious and cautious about her answer.

She bit her lower lip and met his stare. "Jesse was gone for a lot of our marriage,

Ryan," she said in a hushed voice. "It's not as if I didn't have to get used to being alone."

He nodded slowly, unable to unglue his gaze from her lovely face.

"You seem so sad. You took his death really hard, didn't you?" she asked. He was stunned that she seemed more concerned about his well-being than her own.

He felt a muscle flicker in his cheek.

"I do miss Jesse. But his death isn't why I'm feeling so regretful right now."

"Why, then?" she asked shakily, her clear green eyes intent on his face.

Had it been the tremor in her voice that made him do it? Maybe it'd been the mixture of uncertainty and desire shining in her eyes? Whatever it'd been, Ryan couldn't have done anything else in that moment but step forward and take Faith Holmes into his arms.

Chapter Six

They hugged for a long moment. Ryan felt as if he sensed her in every cell of his body, every square inch of his awareness. He wanted like hell to comfort her. He wanted to be utterly confident of her safety and happiness.

She shifted her head and buried her face in his chest, and Ryan forced himself to acknowledge the truth.

He wanted Faith *more than anything. Period.*

She tilted her head back when she felt the slight pressure of his forefinger beneath her chin. Was he really seeing so much unchecked longing in Faith's gaze at that moment? Or was it just what he was feeling reflected in her forest-green eyes?

"No matter how unwise and guilty I feel about it, I can't seem to stop myself from doing this, Faith."

He lowered his head so that their mouths were only inches apart. His gaze moved over her face, reading her reaction to his closeness. Her lips parted as if in anticipation.

He covered her mouth with his own.

The whimper that leaked out of her throat didn't sound distressed, but wondrous. Ryan could completely understand the sentiment. She tasted fantastic. His mouth moved over hers, molding, caressing, shaping her flesh to his...memorizing every sweet nuance of sensation. He sandwiched her lower lip between his, drawing it downward. His tongue slipped between her lips. His first taste was polite, a gentle dip beneath the surface. Then Faith touched him with the tip of her tongue, and her flavor penetrated his consciousness. Heat erupted in him. She glided her tongue against his and sucked lightly, teasing him to come farther...deeper.

He groaned and accepted her invitation wholeheartedly, sweeping his tongue into her mouth.

He cradled her chin at the side of her neck, holding her hostage to his kiss. His fingertips stroked her nape, amazed at her softness. It'd never happened to him before—that a woman's scent and taste could entirely obliterate logic. Apparently it wasn't just a myth, that passion had the ability to burn away rational thought.

She stepped closer and reached around his waist. He made a sound of satisfaction, highly gratified by the feeling of her feminine, firm curves pressing so tightly against him. He put a hand at the small of her back, sealing their bodies into a fit that made everything go black for a moment. Her knees seemed to sag. He broke their kiss and tightened his hold on her waist. He pushed back her dark, coiling hair and pressed his mouth to the side of her neck feverishly.

"Faith," *he whispered roughly.*

"I'm here," *she said.*

A poignant chord struck deep inside his spirit at her two simple words. So generous. So sweet. So inviting to this crazy, but some-

how inevitable experience. She shifted her chin and nuzzled his jaw. Something sharp tore through him. He turned, his mouth finding hers. They fused in a kiss. This time he took her with a raw, elemental hunger that scorched away even the most stubborn lingering doubts and confusion about what was happening to him...what was happening to them.

She arched her back against his hands, offering the soft harbor of her body as a solace to his raging, burning need. The sensation of her breasts crushed against his ribs made him groan. She rubbed against him subtly. He moved in turn, stroking her even as his flesh hardened and thrilled to her sweetness.

He made a rough sound and broke their kiss.

"You're going to think I'm crazy, but when I was over there in that desert, I used to wish like hell you were mine and not Jesse's. How's that for a faithful friend?"

"Ryan," she whispered shakily. "I don't think you're crazy."

She went up on her toes and pressed her mouth to his. A shudder went through him. Suddenly, he was lifting her in his arms. His entire world shifted, until he didn't know left from right, up from down...

...right from wrong.

The only thing Ryan knew as he carried Faith into the living room and laid her on the couch was the recognition of her in the very marrow of his bones...the basic, powerful knowledge that she was his.

He swam in a sea of Faith's fragrance; soft, pale skin; eager, sweet lips and lush, supple curves. If he paused to think about what was happening, he'd stop, and he hated that idea.

Despised it.

He knelt next to the couch. He came down over her, his knees still on the floor, his mouth immediately finding the juncture at her neck and shoulder.

"You smell so good," he muttered, inhaling her scent fully, feeling his blood pound in approval. She moaned softly. He relished the vibrations against his hungry lips. She arched her back. He paused, gritting his teeth at the sensation of full, firm breasts pressing against his chest. He was crazed to touch her, skin to skin. She ran her fingers through his hair, her touch causing prickles of pleasure to course down his neck and spine.

He bracketed her hips with his hands, taking her measure, finding her perfect. His fingers tugged lightly on the belt of her robe at the same time his mouth settled on warm, seeking lips. Her subtle perfume swamped his senses. He wanted to submerse himself in her and never come up for air. He probed the secrets of her mouth, relishing her unique flavor and uncommon responsiveness. She ran her hands beneath his shirt and molded his shoulder muscles into her palms.

The storm raging in his body gripped around flesh and bone, demanding release. He lifted his head a fraction of an inch, but couldn't entirely move away from the sweetest mouth he'd ever tasted.

"Tell me you want me to go away, Faith, because I can't seem to make myself do it," *he muttered next to her damp lips.*

"No. I can't do that," she said. Her fingers traced his neck, and then his collarbone. He tensed when she opened the first, then second button of his shirt and stroked his chest, her fingers avid. He clamped his eyes shut, feeling the inevitability of her touch...the impossibility of denying it.

She leaned forward and caught his mouth

again, plucking at his lips, coaxing and tempting him until he thought he would explode, then and there.

His hands moved on her hips, drawing up her robe and nightgown. When his fingers skimmed the satiny skin of her thighs, he grimaced, need clutching at him with talon-sharp claws. He once again took control of their kiss, ravaging her tenderly. His hand moved, drawing down her panties, finding her heat.

She was soft and warm and wet, and when he touched her, her whimper pierced straight through him.

He never had a logical thought after that point. The world became his hunger. His world became Faith.

He tried to remove his pants, but she held him fast in her kiss, and goodness knows he was too wild for her taste to protest. His need drove at him relentlessly, however. He finally broke their kiss and pressed his mouth against the upper curve of her breast. Her robe had fallen open. Only a layer of thin cotton separated her skin from his caressing lips. She furrowed her fingers through his hair and held him to her as he explored firm, feminine flesh. When he reached the peak of a breast, he took it into his mouth, laving the pebbled, turgid nipple through the fabric.

Her sharp cry was his siren call.

He moved over her, need making him blind to everything but sensation. He felt her wet heat on the tip of his erection and muttered a curse that was a prayer.

"Oh...heavens," he heard her say as if from a great distance. Desire pummeled him, gripping, squeezing...

He drove into her heat, feeling her deepest embrace in every cell of his body.

"Are you all right?" he managed between a clenched jaw. He pried open his eyelids. The vision of Faith laying there while they were fused, her dark hair spread on the cushion, her lovely face tight and glazed with desire, was scorched into his brain...quite possibly for an eternity.

She reached for him, her fervent kiss his answer.

The buzzing sound of his cell phone interrupted his heated memories. Ryan glanced at the number, scowling, and hit the receive button.

"Hey," Ryan greeted his sister gruffly.

"Did I wake you up?" Mari, his sister, asked.

"No, I was watching the Tigers game. I'm going to drive over to the airport here in a bit to meet with the owner of a Cessna I want to buy. What's up?"

"I just wanted to confirm lunch tomorrow. Did Faith say she'd come?"

Ryan and Mari had been close growing up, but the sudden, tragic loss of their parents when Mari was eighteen and Ryan was twenty had tightened their bond even more. He could hear the threads of anxiety and excitement in his sister's voice at the prospect of meeting Faith. When he'd told his sister last night about Faith and the pregnancy, she'd first expressed her worry about how he was handling things. After she'd listened to him describe Faith, however, excitement had started to filter into her voice.

"She'll be there. Are you sure you should make the trip?" Ryan asked, standing and turning off the television.

Mari laughed. In his mind's eye he could clearly see the droll roll of her whiskey-colored eyes. "I think I'm up to the hour drive from Chicago to Harbor Town. You'd better get used to the idea that a pregnant woman isn't disabled, Ryan."

"Between you and Faith constantly telling me, I'll likely learn the lesson soon enough," he mumbled dryly as he pulled a shirt out of the closet.

"Good. Faith sounds like she'll keep you in line. Can you pick me up at Brigit's? I wouldn't ask, but I promised to meet with Deidre about the project she's started for veterans with post-traumatic stress syndrome at the center," Mari explained. She referred to The Family Center, the innovative community and treatment center for survivors of substance abuse that Mari had begun several years ago. Mari, the Reyes family, and all of the Kavanaugh children were intimately involved in the funding and workings of The Family Center, since all of them were direct survivors of substance abuse. Members of all three families had lost family members following a car wreck caused by Derry Kavanaugh when he'd been driving drunk seventeen years ago.

"Yeah, I wanted to double check with Deidre that she's all squared away with Scott to fly to Tahoe tomorrow, anyway," he said. "I'll pick you up at twelve-thirty," Ryan said before he bid her goodbye and hung up the phone.

He finished dressing, intent on going to the airport and finalizing the details for his purchase of the new plane for Eagle Air.

He only hoped Faith hadn't changed her mind about agreeing to come tomorrow.

Faith stood in her backyard the following morning watching Topsy poke her nose into every possible crevice she could. She soaked up the warm sunshine, glorying in the first bona fide springlike day of the year.

"Faith?"

She spun around at the sound of the deep voice calling from the front of the house. "Ryan, I'm back here!"

He came around the side of the house a moment later. She waited, appreciating the sight of him while he approached. He wore a pair of canvas pants along with a button-down blue-and-white twill shirt. Both items of clothing fitted him perfectly, highlighting long legs, narrow hips and the appealing slant of his torso from a lean waist to a powerful chest and shoulders.

He looked good enough to eat.

Recognizing her errant thought, she plastered a smile on her face as he opened the fence gate and approached her.

"You got here quicker than I'd expected. I thought I better let Topsy out before we left."

"There wasn't any traffic in town. I got here fast," he said, his dark eyes moving over her. She felt her cheeks warming beneath what appeared to be an appreciative male appraisal. "Isn't this weather amazing? The first real day of spring," she said breathlessly.

"You look like springtime," he murmured, his stare sweeping over her floral-colored skirt and lingering on the front of her light-weight peach-colored sweater.

"Thanks," she managed. Something about his low, gruff voice made her already warm cheeks burn. She'd purchased some spring-time items for her wardrobe, well aware that her breasts were growing past the confines of her prepregnancy blouses. Even this new sweater seemed to highlight her growing curves, however. Ryan's appreciative glance didn't offend her like it would have if another man had perused her in such a manner.

In fact, his warm glance made her feel downright...desirable...

...aroused.

"Topsy!" she called, eager to derail her potentially dangerous train of thought. The puppy glanced around at her call and suddenly tore through the yard. She immediately went to Ryan, wiggling and hopping around his ankles. Ryan grinned and bent to pet the caramel-colored fluff ball, scratching Topsy behind the ears until she literally vibrated with pleasure.

"You've made a friend for life," Faith said, enjoying watching Ryan's long fingers stroke the puppy. No wonder Topsy appeared to be in a state of bliss. What was it about seeing a big, masculine man with something so tiny and adorable that appealed so much to a woman? A strange, powerful feeling tightened her chest.

What would it be like to see him hold their child?

"You think so?" Ryan asked, picking up Topsy and holding her in front of his face, examining the canine soberly. Faith burst out in laughter at the comical sound he made when Topsy lapped at his nose with a pink tongue.

"Why are you so quiet?" Ryan asked her several minutes later when they were on the road to Harbor Town.

"I'm worried about meeting your sister," Faith admitted, staring at the sun-gilded, blooming trees and meadows zooming past the car window.

"She'll love you. There's absolutely nothing to worry about."

"Easy for you to say," Faith said quietly. She glanced at Ryan when he reached across the console and put his hand on top of hers where it'd been resting on her thigh. His heat soaked down into her skin.

"It is easy for me to say, because I know Mari, and I know you. What specifically are you worried about?"

Faith bit at her lower lip, hesitant to reveal her insecurities. Ryan tightened his hold on her hand, as if in reassurance.

"I know it's ridiculous," she murmured, watching as they passed the city limit sign for Harbor Town. "I'm thirty years old, not a teenager, but I can't help but feel like she might think I'm...some kind of a..."

"What?" Ryan prodded when she faded off.

"Loose woman," Faith burst out. It sounded so ridiculous when she said it, she couldn't help but give Ryan a sheepish grin. He wore an incredulous expression that segued to amusement.

"*Loose woman?* This isn't the 1950s, Faith. Lots of women have babies who aren't married, or even in a serious relationship."

"I know. Maybe loose isn't the word. Maybe stupid is. Women in this day and age aren't supposed to get pregnant after a...a..." She struggled to finish her sentence, becoming increasingly uncomfortable when she couldn't. When Ryan released her hand, she looked at him in alarm. Had she offended him? She hadn't meant to minimize Christmas Eve, she just didn't know how to describe what had happened between them.

Still.

"Mari isn't going to judge you," he said as he stared out the front window and drove. "She's not a judgmental person, in the first place, and in the second place, there's nothing to judge. She's as aware as anyone that you can't always plan life. You just live it as best you can."

Faith inhaled slowly, studying his profile. He turned into a residential neighborhood featuring a tree-lined street and attractive older large homes. Of course he was right. How could she possibly feel the tiniest shame about the miracle of life growing inside her?

Ryan brought the car to a crawl.

"See that house there?" he asked, pointing to a lovely sprawling residence complete with a sweeping porch and swing that had been built in the Arts and Crafts style and lovingly restored. "That was our summer house."

"It's beautiful," Faith breathed. "Isn't there a beach down at the end of the street?" she asked, pointing to a wooded cul-de-sac. "What a wonderful neighborhood for kids this must have been."

"Yeah, the beach is on the other side of those trees. We lived on that beach during the summer. A bunch of the parents on the street conspired to serve dinner at the same time every night so that only one of them had to go down to round us all up for supper," Ryan said, smiling in memory.

"It's for sale," Faith said, pointing at the sign in the yard.

Ryan did a double take and frowned. "Mari and I just sold it to a couple a little over a year ago. They must have had a change of heart."

A moment later Ryan turned into the driveway of an appealing white-shingled Colonial Revival-style home. He put the car in Park, but instead of getting out, he turned toward her, his intent manner taking her off guard.

"If it bothers you that much, the idea of being single and having the baby—"

He paused, leaving Faith puzzled as to what he was about to say, his gaze fixed out the front windshield. Faith saw a beautiful woman with long dark hair coming down the front steps of the house toward them. She wore an attractive green dress that tied beneath her breasts and above the small roundness of her belly. Her leather lace-up sandals and matching shoulder bag gave her a hip, sophisticated appearance. As she approached the car, Ryan's sister smiled at Faith through the window. Faith stepped out of the car to greet her.

Within a minute of meeting Mari Kavanaugh, Faith fully recognized how baseless her fears were. Mari was one of the warmest, kindest people she'd ever met. The fact that she seemed as eager to know Faith as Faith was to know her helped matters greatly.

The three of them ate outdoors on the patio at a local restaurant, Jake's Place. The weather was ideal, the company excellent and the food good. Mari and Faith compared notes on their pregnancy while Ryan listened. Despite his impassive expression, Faith thought he paid close attention to what they said. It was obvious to Faith that Ryan deeply cared about his little sister. He leaned forward and took part in the conversation more animatedly when the topic turned to Mari's daughter, Riley. It warmed her heart to hear him speak with such fond pride of his niece.

"That's the last one I have on my cell phone," Ryan said as he showed Faith the final photo, this one of a grinning little girl sitting amongst a huge pile of torn Christmas wrapping, a red wrapping bow in her curly, dark hair.

"She liked the wrapping paper more than she did her presents," Mari told Faith with a twinkle in her eyes.

"She's absolutely adorable," Faith said sincerely, handing the phone back to Ryan. "Do you and your husband know if Riley is going to have a brother or sister?"

"A sister," Mari said, giving Ryan a knowing glance. "Another niece for Uncle Ryan to spoil. Speaking of which, what about *you*? Am I going to have a niece or nephew? My first time being an aunt!" Mari said with barely contained excitement.

Faith laughed. Mari's enthusiasm was contagious. The two women began talking excitedly, pausing to nod an acknowledgment when Ryan saw an old friend walk onto the patio and excused himself to go and greet him. Mari watched her brother walk away and glanced at Faith with a smile.

"He probably needs a break from all the estrogen we're exuding."

Faith chuckled, but shook her head a little sadly. She caught Mari's eye.

"He's got to be plowed under by all this, Mari. It was the last thing he expected."

Mari's grin faded. She reached across the table and patted Faith's hand. "The same must be true for you," she said feelingly.

"I'm okay," she assured. "You know how it is, being a mother. Sure, it took me by storm when I realized I was going to have a baby. But I've had months to come to terms with it, and the baby is here—" she touched her belly significantly "—growing inside me. It's different for Ryan."

"He'll get his footing. Ryan is nothing if not adaptable. He may be stunned, but he's also happy, Faith. Incredibly so," Mari added more quietly.

"Do you really think so?"

Mari nodded. "I could hear the wonder in his voice when he told me he was going to have a child. Family is very important to Ryan."

"I can imagine." Faith's expression tightened with compassion and she turned her hand, giving Mari's hand a squeeze. "You guys lost your family when you were so young. It's no wonder he values family ties the way he does. Did he…did Ryan tell you about his plans to move to Michigan?" Faith asked hesitantly.

Mari's golden brown eyes filled with concern. "I'm guessing you're not very pleased about that?"

"It's not that," Faith exclaimed. "His decision just took me by surprise, that's all." She sighed and leaned back in her chair. "To be honest, this whole thing with your brother has taken me off guard."

"I can only imagine. At least one little mystery has been cleared up for me," Mari said, a small smile tugging at her mouth.

"What's that?"

"Why Ryan was so fixed and determined to return to Michigan last Christmas Eve. I thought for sure he'd be less than thrilled at the idea of spending the holiday at Brigit's house, so I was shocked when he readily— even eagerly—agreed to come with us to Harbor Town. He obviously was looking forward to seeing you."

Faith's eyes widened in amazement at this news. Perhaps Mari noticed her unsettlement because she gave her a big smile.

"Like I said, time is what's needed. You two will figure things out. For my part, I'm thrilled to have met you."

"I'm so glad to have met you, as well," she returned sincerely. "I was really worried about it, earlier."

"Why?" Mari asked.

"I thought you might…you know…judge

me for being pregnant when I'm not even dating your brother," she mumbled.

"Don't be silly. I'm the last person on earth to judge something like that. I hadn't seen Riley's father—Marc—for a decade when I accidentally got pregnant. We can't always plan life. We just have to—"

"Live it," Faith finished for her, repeating what Ryan had said in the car earlier.

Mari squeezed her hand before she let it go. "Babies are amazing things all on their own, but what's truly wonderful is the way they can pull people together," Mari said meaningfully before she glanced toward the far side of the patio. Faith followed the path of her gaze and saw Ryan walking toward them, his stare directly on her. Her heart began to pound erratically.

"That definitely sounds like the case with you and your husband," Faith said hesitantly. "It's different for Ryan and I. Our situation is…unusual."

"Babies also have a way of making the unusual more commonplace," Mari assured.

Faith smiled shakily. The baby was already bringing Ryan and her closer. It excited her to be near him, to feel his admiring glances and warm touches...to feel like an attractive, desirable woman again.

But what if they got *too* close?

Eventually, he'd fly away from her. He'd live a life separate from her as he traveled with his charter airline. He'd sleep in strange beds...possibly with strange women? The life of a pilot's wife was uncertain, lonely...unsecure. That was an experience she could not allow herself to repeat.

So why, Faith wondered anxiously as she watched Ryan come toward them, his gaze unwavering on her, did Ryan strike her as a veritable mountain of stability? Solid. Enduring.

When they dropped Mari off at Brigit Kavanaugh's later, Faith saw two women swaying on the front porch swing and recognized one of them.

"Would you mind very much if I went and said hello to Brigit?" Faith asked Ryan.

"No, of course not."

Before she got out of the car, she turned toward the backseat. "Did you by chance tell Brigit? About the baby?" she asked Mari.

Mari shook her head.

"Thank you. I'd rather not get into it right

now, if that's all right with you?" she asked Ryan.

"Fine with me," Ryan stated. Something in his tone told Faith that he couldn't have agreed more with her decision. She recalled what Mari had said about how she'd expected Ryan to resist going to Brigit's house last Christmas Eve. It couldn't be easy for him, spending time in the house that was once owned by the man who had killed his parents in a case of involuntary manslaughter. How did he feel about his sister marrying Marc Kavanaugh, Derry Kavanaugh's oldest son?

Faith put her concerns on hold when Brigit came to the top of the steps to greet her a moment later, a smile on her face and her arms outstretched. The pretty older woman gave her a warm hug.

"Imagine my surprise when Mari told me this morning she was having lunch with Faith Holmes!" Brigit exclaimed.

"I thought the same thing when Ryan mentioned you," Faith replied happily. She was glad to see Brigit looking so well. She was always attractive and well put together, but Faith had never seen her in such good spirits. She turned and saw the stunning young woman who had come to stand beside her mother, and wondered if Brigit's glow wasn't related to her. Brigit had mentioned once that Deidre and she had been estranged since the accident, but here they were, side by side, both of them smiling. The two women were an older and younger version of one another.

"You must be Deidre," Faith said, holding out her hand to Brigit's daughter. "Your mother has told me so much about you. I'm Faith."

"It's nice to meet you," Deidre said, glancing from Faith to Ryan with friendly curiosity.

They stayed and chatted for half an hour. When they finally stood to leave, Faith promised to keep in touch with Mari and they exchanged phone numbers.

"Let Nick know I'll be calling him next week. I have some important news to discus with him," Ryan told Deidre as they were leaving. Nick Malone was the CEO of Du-Bois Enterprises and Deidre's husband. The Malones had contracted Eagle Air for piloting services for their multibillion-dollar company, but Faith got the impression the couple and Ryan respected and liked each other.

Deidre's gaze flickered over Faith when Ryan took her hand as they stood on the stairs. "When do I get to hear this news?" she asked with a teasing grin.

"You know as well as I do that as soon as I tell Nick, you'll know, as well," Ryan grumbled dryly. "But I'll call you next week, as well."

"Good. You know I don't like to feel left out," Deidre joked, waving as they walked toward the car.

"That was nice," Faith murmured later as they drove back to Holland. "You were right about Mari. She's wonderful. It was nice to see Brigit, as well."

"Yeah. It was. Nice, I mean," Ryan said. She glanced at him in surprise, his tone had been so steadfast.

"I had the impression Brigit wasn't one of your favorite people."

"She didn't used to be," Ryan admitted, his gaze on the road. "The lawsuits that followed the accident years ago sort of put the Kavanaughs and us on opposite sides of the ring. It wasn't pretty."

"I can only imagine," Faith said, compassion filling her when she considered what people on all sides must have suffered following such a horrific accident. Ryan glanced at her quickly, a small smile on his face.

"But I have to admit…seeing how fond Brigit was of you, I have a new respect for her. She was doing what I wanted to do all along—making sure you were okay and safe and sound. I appreciate her in a whole new way for being here and looking out for you."

She opened her mouth to remind him she was very capable of looking out for herself, but halted. He'd sounded so warm and thoughtful just now, it was difficult to find fault in what he'd said. Was it really such a terrible thing that he worried about her, even though it was unwarranted? Didn't that mean he cared…even a little?

"Would you like to come in?" she asked him when he pulled into her driveway, damning her breathlessness.

"I would, if you don't mind," he said. "I brought my tape measure. I was hoping to get some measurements for the bookcases so that I can start coming up with a sketch for you. We can bounce ideas off that."

"That'd be terrific," she said, watching as

he reached in the backseat for a tape measure, ruler and a tablet of paper.

He immediately went into the nursery-to-be and began working. Faith let Topsy out into the backyard and fed the cats. She walked into the baby's room a half hour later. Ryan sat on the only chair in the room, the sketch-pad open on his spread thighs. She peered over his shoulder at his sketch.

"It's just preliminary, but what would you think about something like this?" he asked, his pencil still moving over the paper. He moved aside the ruler to show her what he'd drawn. Fascinated, Faith sunk to her knees next to him, her forearms braced on the arms of his chair.

"Oh, that'd be amazing, Ryan," she enthused, admiring the multi-unit shelving and cabinet unit. "I can't believe you came up with that so quickly. I love it."

He waved his pencil over the two corner benches. "These can be used for both sitting and for toy storage, and these cabinets can hold anything from sports equipment to clothing to diapers. Then there's the book shelves, for displaying things and—"

"Books. Lots and lots of books."

Ryan glanced at her. Their heads were close enough that Faith could easily see the warm gleam in his eyes. She also could smell his clean, spicy scent. She breathed deeper, as if she wanted to absorb it.

"I'm glad you think books are so important," he said quietly.

"Of course I do."

She couldn't pull her gaze off his lips when they twitched in a smile. He leaned closer to her. She couldn't seem to stop herself from craning closer to him, until their mouths were only inches apart. He still watched her intently. She saw his nostrils flare, as if he was trying to capture her scent as she had his. Her heart stalled, and then began to race.

"I should have known that learning would be a top priority for a straight-A student."

"Don't forget gym class."

"I'm not forgetting anything," he said before his lips brushed against hers.

Chapter Seven

It was more of a gentle, skimming caress than a kiss, as if he was curious as to how her mouth felt and used his own to discover the information. Faith closed her eyes and just experienced him; firm, warm, fragrant flesh sliding and rubbing against her own sensitive, tingling lips. She pressed closer, eager for more of the sensation of him, molding her mouth against his, hungrier now…blindly seeking.

He put his hand on the back of her head and pierced her lips with his tongue. Excitement knifed through her, sharp and compelling.

Her nipples prickled and tightened. A gnawing ache expanded at her core, a feeling she knew from experience that Ryan could build and mount in her flesh...and finally vanquish in a delicious rush of pure pleasure.

A loud, high-pitched wail penetrated her haze of arousal. Ryan closed their kiss and leaned back slightly, a mixture of alarm and puzzlement on his face.

"It's Topsy," she said in an apologetic tone. She snorted into soft laughter when the comically mournful howling continued. Faith pushed up on the arm of Ryan's chair and stood. "I'll just go and get her. I left her out in the yard."

"Her Highness doesn't like to be left waiting," Ryan said, grinning, although the embers of arousal remained in his eyes.

Thinking it was best to get some distance from him for a bit, considering how much she'd lost herself in that kiss, Faith busied herself in other rooms for the next several minutes. When she walked down the hallway to her bedroom a while later, Topsy panting after her on her heels, she noticed he was still in the baby's room, absorbed in his task. She entered her room and closed the door, leaving it open a crack. She quickly undressed and pulled on some jeans. Standing in her opened closet door, she searched for a blouse to wear, her hands skimming over several garments. Her fingers paused on the hanger for her evening dress that she planned to wear for the benefit Wednesday night for the Animal Advocates Alliance.

Impulsively she pulled out the dress and closed her closet door, peering into the mirror on the other side. It was a champagne-colored sleeveless silk number that she'd purchased last October, before she was pregnant. She held up the dress to the front of her body, her brow furrowed in worry. It was a tasteful dress, but more low-cut than Faith typically wore her necklines. She hadn't considered before—what if her slightly pregnancy-swollen breasts would be too obvious in the dress?

A knock sounded on her door. She started.

"Faith?"

"Yes?"

Ryan poked his head around the door. Faith's heart did a flip-flop. She plastered the dress over the front of her. Ryan's gaze immediately dropped and widened.

"I'm sorry. I didn't mean to—" He paused

and cleared his throat. "I was just coming to say goodbye."

"Oh, okay. Let me pull something on and I'll see you out," she said in a high-pitched voice.

His glance lowered again. "That's very pretty," he said, referring to the evening gown.

"Thanks. It's for the ball next Wednesday," she said, gathering herself a bit. It wasn't as if he could really *see* anything, with the dress held up over her mostly bare torso. This is what she told herself, anyway, when he stepped into the room. It struck her how large he appeared to be in her feminine retreat—how male. He came toward her and paused a few feet away, examining the dress.

"You'll look fantastic in that," he said.

She gave an awkward laugh. "I hope it fits. I was just wondering about that. I bought it when I wasn't pregnant. I'll probably be a total disaster."

He met her stare. "You won't be."

"How do you know?"

Instead of answering her, he calmly put his hand on the dress hanger. Faith released it hesitantly when he pulled. He tossed the gown over a nearby chair and put his hands on her shoulders. He turned her so that she faced the mirror and stood behind her.

Faith couldn't breathe.

"Look at you," Ryan said.

She inhaled with effort. He was following his own command, his eyes smoldering as they traveled over her image in the mirror. He placed his opened hand on her bare waist. Tendrils of pleasure curled through her belly when he moved it, sliding his palm over her hip and abdomen. His stare looked hot and worshipful as they both watched him touch her.

"I know Jesse pulled a number on you, but it's time you saw reality," he said quietly, his mouth near her right ear. She shivered when his fingers gently detailed her rib cage, his dark hand an erotic contrast to her pale skin. "You're a beautiful, sexy woman. Are you looking?" he asked, nudging her hair with his nose. His fingers coasted along the tender skin at her sides. She bit her lower lip to stifle a gasp.

"Yes," she managed.

"But are you *seeing*?" He stepped closer. She felt his groin brush against the top of her backside. "Flawless, soft skin," he murmured, stroking the inner part of her elbow.

He palmed her hip. "Curves that fit my hand perfectly." His fingers traveled up the center of her rib cage, and then detoured to the left, tracing the skin beneath the cloth of her white bra. She couldn't take her gaze off the image of them in the mirror. Heat coursed through her. "Delicate and narrow in all the right places." He stepped closer as he caressed the sensitive skin, pressing his front more fully to her bottom. He brought his other hand around her and palmed both of her breasts, lifting slightly as if to test their weight.

A shaky sigh escaped her throat.

"Curvy and full in all the other ones," he added, his voice now low and husky. His fingertips flickered over her nipples, making them tighten against the clinging fabric of her bra. He made a low, rough sound of male appreciation. Much to her disappointment, however, he released her breasts. His hands gathered her hair and pulled it behind her shoulders.

"Hair a man wants to sink his fingers into," he continued, sliding his hands along her shoulders and collarbone. He traced the line of her jaw, his stare on her intense. "And a face that haunts a man's dreams."

For a few seconds he remained still. They examined one another in the mirror while the air burned in Faith's lungs.

"At least this man's dreams," he added with a small, sheepish smile. He moved against her ever so slightly, leaving her in little doubt of his desire.

"Faith?"

"Yes?" she managed to whisper, even though her body was buzzing with sexual awareness and she was utterly entranced by Ryan's stare.

"Do you have a date to the ball on Wednesday?"

She started slightly. It hadn't been what she expected him to say.

"No," she blurted out before she had a chance to censor herself.

"I'd like to take you."

"Okay."

What else could she say, with such a gorgeous man pressed against her, hot and aroused? No sane woman could have resisted his smoky-eyed, wanting stare that seemed to promise untold sensual delights.

He leaned down and pressed his face to the side of her neck. A shudder of excitement went through her at the sensation of his warm lips moving against her skin.

Then he straightened and the hard pressure of his body was gone.

"Ryan?" she asked uncertainly when he stepped away.

"If I don't leave now, I'm not going to, Faith," he said, his voice sounding edgy. He glanced around, spearing her with his stare. His expression softened.

"I'll call you on Tuesday and we can make plans," he said. He briefly caressed her shoulder, turned and walked out of the room, leaving Faith standing there alone, a vibrating bundle of confusion and clamoring nerves.

On Wednesday at five-thirty Faith raced through her front door, laden down with dry cleaning, her briefcase and a large bag of dog chow. Topsy's loud yipping added another layer of chaos to her already overwhelmed state.

"I'm coming, I'm coming," she muttered in a regretful tone, dumping all the items she carried on the breakfast nook. Both Cleo and Smokey circled around her feet, meowing loudly for their supper. "I'm sorry for being late. My hair appointment had to be rescheduled because I had a patient emergency—an Irish setter managed to consume a jumbo package of toilet paper, including the plastic. Don't you ever think about pulling something like that, young lady," she lectured a squirming Topsy as she liberated her from her crate. The puppy shot like a torpedo through the back door when she opened it. She gave the cats their dinner in record time.

She only had a half an hour to get ready before Ryan would be here. Luckily, she'd gone to the salon in town to get her hair done, so the only thing that was required was a quick shower and makeup application.

At six o'clock, she stood in front of the bathroom mirror, inspecting the final result. Her skin looked smooth and glowing next to the champagne fabric of the dress. Her hairdresser had straightened her hair, and then used a curling iron to create loose curls that spilled down her shoulders and caressed her bare upper arms. The dress gathered beneath her breasts and then flowed in graceful folds to below her knees. Nervousness trickled through her when she saw the amount of cleavage revealed in the V-shape of the neckline. Was it entirely appropriate? She'd tried the dress on for Jane last night, however, and her friend had insisted it fit her perfectly.

"With curves like that, you ought to be flaunting it a little. It'll only help in getting a little extra cash from the male attendees during the silent auction you're running," Jane had said, her blue eyes twinkling. Faith had stood before a mirror at Jane's house while they both inspected her appearance. "And I doubt you'll hear that hunk of a man I met the other day in the office complaining."

After that it'd taken Jane about three seconds flat to get her to admit that Ryan Itani was, indeed, the father of her baby. When Jane had seen Faith's worried expression, she'd expressed confusion.

"Why are you upset that you're about to have that man's baby? He's gorgeous, and I saw the way he looked at you—like he wanted to eat you up in one bite. What's the problem?"

"Which one do you want me to start with?" Faith had asked drolly. She noticed Jane's mock stern expression in the mirror. *"He's not in love with me or anything. That night— it was all a mistake...an impulse."*

"Seems to me that your impulses are pretty good," Jane said dryly as she'd adjusted the bodice at Faith's back.

"He's not a one-woman man," Faith said, scowling at her reflection in the mirror. "Look at his job. Pilots live out of their suitcases. There's no...security in a man like that."

"Who are you talking about?" Jane asked, her gaze sharp in the mirror. "Ryan? Or Jesse?"

Faith sighed. Jane knew all about the heartache her former husband had caused her. "It doesn't matter. Ryan's not interested in me that way." Her cheeks grew pink when Jane gave her a *give me a break* glance. "I mean...he's attracted to me. But he also told me he wants us to be friends."

Jane had just shrugged in a matter-of-fact manner. "Lust and friendship aren't a bad way to start, I'd say. Add a baby into the mix, and you've got the beginnings of a beautiful relationship."

A loud knock sounded on her front door, causing Faith to jump and jerking her out of her thoughts. She spun toward the vanity, the decadently soft folds of the skirt of the dress whisking around her hips and thighs. She tossed some money, a credit card, a comb and lipstick into her evening bag and hurried down the hallway, her heart starting to hammer out an erratic tempo in her ears.

Ryan had called yesterday, and they'd chatted for a few minutes. Other than that brief interaction, however, she hadn't had contact with him since last Sunday, when he'd touched her while they'd looked at one another in the mirror...when he'd *praised* her.

When he'd coaxed her into seeing herself in a whole new way.

"Hi," she greeted between pants a few seconds later, opening the outer door. Ryan caught it with his hand. Her frazzled brain fully took in his appearance for the first time. She froze, her eyes going wide.

"Oh, my goodness," she exclaimed. "You look great."

It was a bit of an understatement, she thought as her gaze ran over the considerable length of him.

It was a *lot* of an understatement.

He wore a classic black tux, white dress shirt with wing collar, points tucked behind a black bow tie. Faith always thought he looked completely natural wearing casual clothing and his leather flight jacket. She realized for the first time that he was so magnetically handsome, he could probably pull off wearing a paper bag.

Seeing him in an immaculate tuxedo was like a sock to the gut.

"You look amazing, yourself," Ryan said, his gaze going over her warmly.

"Where did you get that tuxedo?" she wondered incredulously. The elegant garment fit his large, lean body too well to have been anything but tailor made for him.

"I flew over to Chicago and had a rush job done on it. I needed to buy one anyway," Ryan said. "Since I've started working for Nick and Deidre, they've invited me to a few formal events. I needed a tux."

Faith realized she was standing there gaping at him while he stood on her front steps, holding the door.

"I'm sorry. Please come in. I just have to get my wrap." She flew to the kitchen, where she retrieved the pale, fluid evening wrap she'd had dry-cleaned. When she rejoined

Ryan, her wrap draped over her arm, she saw that he carried a small plastic container.

"This is for you," he said, handing it to her.

Her eyes sprang wide. "A corsage?"

"No," he said. "It's just a single orchid. I thought it'd look great in your hair. If it doesn't, though, you can just put it in a vase."

"Oh, Ryan," she said, staring at the single, gorgeous bloom resting in the container. For some odd reason, her eyes smarted with tears. He'd recalled the color of her gown from last weekend, when he'd walked in and she'd been holding it up in the mirror. That such a masculine man remembered such a small detail and translated that knowledge into such a perfect gift struck a deep emotional chord in her. She looked at him.

"Thank you. I *will* wear it in my hair. You got the color exactly. Give me just a second," she said, beaming at him before she hurried to the bathroom to find a pin to affix the orchid.

He couldn't have chosen better. The champagne-colored bloom looked lovely next to her dark hair. She removed the necklace she'd put on, allowing the flower to be her only accent besides a small pair of diamond studs in her ears.

His eyes seemed to glow when she joined him a second later.

"You're right. It is perfect," he said, smiling. He dipped his dark head and kissed her on the mouth, brief and electric.

Her breathing didn't return to normal until they were seated in the car and halfway to the Lake View restaurant.

"I hope you won't be too bored," Faith said worriedly when he pulled into the packed parking lot. "As the Alliance president I'll have to speak, and I'm responsible for the silent auction. The auction and cocktail party starts at six-thirty, and the dinner will follow. A couple of people from the board will be helping me do some last-minute things, so—"

"I'll be fine. You just do whatever you have to do," Ryan assured. She glanced over at his profile, sensing his calm confidence, and realized that of course he'd be fine. He was nothing if not self-sufficient.

She was aware of him all evening, despite the fact that she put considerable effort into socializing with all the guests during the combined cocktail hour and silent auction. He was at least a head taller than most of the attendees at the fundraiser, so it was easy to spot him above the crowd. He did, indeed, appear to be comfortable, meeting and chatting with strangers. Once she observed him talking to Sheila Maxwell, a local attorney. They made quite a striking pair standing next to each other, sipping their drinks, chatting and laughing. Jealousy made an unwanted appearance, swelling in her belly. It ducked its ugly head when she noticed that Ryan spoke just as long, and just as animatedly, to Mortimer Cohen, a wealthy octogenarian, as he had the statuesque Sheila.

She lost sight of him when the lights dimmed in the large dining room in order to show the brief film about the charitable work of the Animal Advocate Alliance.

"Those are your hands holding that dog. I'd recognize them anywhere," a deep voice said quietly in her right ear.

Faith turned around and saw Ryan's shadowed face just over her right shoulder. She smiled.

"You're amazing. I hadn't realized there was anything singular about my hands," she said, referring to the video that detailed the experience of one homeless dog from when it'd been taken in by the Alliance to when it had eventually been adopted by a family. Faith was shown in the video giving the canine a medical exam and providing its shots, although her face didn't appear on camera.

"I recognized your touch."

She blinked at having those sweet, intimate words murmured in her ear. She struggled to recover.

"Are you having an okay time?" she whispered.

"Yes. And I happen to know from mingling with your guests that you've got a ton of donations coming your way. I'm hoping the night will be a big success," he said quietly near her ear.

She craned her head around, trying to see him better in the shadowed room. "Thank you, Ryan."

She just made out his small smile and the gleam in his eyes before the video presentation ended and the lights came back up. Reluctantly Faith excused herself to call everyone to dinner and give her speech.

Afterward she sat down next to Ryan at the head table and gave a sigh of relief.

"It's finished. The hard part is over," she

whispered, since another committee member now spoke at the podium.

"Congratulations for a job well done," he said quietly. She gratefully accepted the glass of ice water Ryan handed her. "I'd make it champagne, but under the circumstances..." He faded off, glancing down over her stomach.

"Water is just perfect," she said, sharing a smile with him.

After they'd finished their meal, a four-man band began to play music and couples moved onto the dance floor.

"What do you think? Are you too wiped out to dance?" Ryan asked, nodding toward the dance floor, which was situated directly in front of floor-to-ceiling windows and an outdoor terrace that overlooked the lake and the setting sun.

"I'd love to," Faith said.

She took his hand and they joined several other couples on the floor. He took her into his arms and they might have been the only people alive on the planet.

"Another gorgeous sunset," he murmured, even though his stare was on her face, not on the brilliant palette of streaking color in the western sky.

"Yes. It's nice. For the fundraiser, I mean," Faith breathed. "You're pretty light on your feet for a flyboy."

"You're not a bad dancer yourself, for a C-minus gym student," he replied, his mouth twitching in a grin. She laughed. He pulled her closer, sealing their fronts together, her breasts pressing against his ribs. His nostrils flared slightly as he looked down at her. She couldn't pull her gaze off him.

"Remember the other day, when you said that an adrenaline rush wasn't your main reason for becoming a pilot?" she asked. He nodded. "What *was* the primary reason, then?"

He studied her face silently for a moment before he responded.

"It's kind of hard to put into words," he said eventually.

"Try me."

"Okay. The first time I ever flew in a plane, it was on a commercial airliner to Hawaii with my family. I was seven. I'll never forget it—the brute force of the plane lifting me, looking out the window and seeing an entire new world. It didn't hit me immediately that my mom and dad and sister weren't as blown away by the whole thing as I was. For me it was like a religious experience or something. I just *knew* I was meant to be up there."

Faith stared at him for a moment, touched by the force of his conviction.

"Do you miss it a lot? When you're...you know. On the ground?"

"Since I entered the academy, I was usually never on the ground long enough to go through withdrawal."

"I'd like to see you fly," she said. "I'd like to see you in your element."

"Name the day," he said quietly. She felt him studying her as she looked out at the radiant sunset as they slowly spun on the dance floor.

"Does it bother you?" he asked.

"What?" she asked, puzzled.

"That I love flying so much."

"Of course not. It's wonderful that you're so passionate about your job."

His gaze narrowed on her. "You're not being entirely honest. You associate a love of flying with an impermanent character."

She dropped her chin, looking sightlessly at his immaculate white shirt.

"Faith?"

"Yes?" she asked with false cheerfulness.

"Look at me," he said.

She slowly lifted her head and met his stare. It annoyed her that she found the topic so charged. What did it matter to her that Ryan had a passion for the freedom of the open skies?

"Maybe the reason I always got so homesick when I wasn't flying was that I never really had a permanent home after my parents died. I lived all over the globe in my years in the military. A plane became my refuge. That doesn't mean I can't eventually find a refuge somewhere else someday."

"On the ground?" She glanced out the floor-to-ceiling windows again, not wanting him to see the doubt in her yes.

"Yeah. On the ground. I don't think I'll ever stop loving to fly, but it's possible to feel at home in more than one place, isn't it?"

She put on a brave face and nodded. "Of course it is."

She was glad when the music came to an end. She had a feeling from Ryan's narrowed gaze that he didn't really believe her convicted tone. He tugged on her hand when she started to return to their seats at the table.

"Let's get your wrap and step onto the terrace for a moment," he said.

"Okay," Faith replied. Her heart started to do a drumroll on her breastbone as he led her out onto the empty terrace. The sun had sunk completely into Lake Michigan at this point, leaving a lingering residue of pink, purple and gold streaks in the western sky.

"What is it, Ryan?" Faith asked when they faced one another next to the rail of the terrace and she saw how somber his expression was. A chilly lake breeze swept past them. Faith shivered and pulled her wrap closer around her. Before she suspected what he planned, Ryan took her into his arms. She stiffened at first, but then found herself melting against him. She sighed, pressing her cheek to his lapel. The fortress of his embrace felt wonderful—solid, warm and secure.

"There's something important we need to talk about," he said. She became distracted when she felt him press his mouth to the top of her head, kissing her.

"What?" she asked, something in his serious tone making her wary.

"We need to talk about the baby—its security, both legally and financially."

Faith swallowed and lifted her head. She could just make out his stark features in the dim light from the restaurant.

"All right," she said. "What about it?"

He reached up and gently removed a windblown curl from her cheek. She shivered, but not from cold, when he tucked it behind her ear and his fingers grazed her skin.

"The thing of it is, Faith," he began, "given the circumstances, I think the right thing to do—the *only* thing to do—is for us to get married."

Chapter Eight

From her stunned expression of disbelief, Ryan realized it'd been the last thing she'd expected him to say. He felt himself sinking and forced himself to rally. He'd known this particular challenge wouldn't be easy.

"You can't be serious," she said.

"I'm dead serious. Think about it, Faith. If we marry, I'll have a legal responsibility for the child, no matter what."

Anxiety leaked into her expression. "You need it to be a *legal obligation* to be a father to the baby?"

"No. That's not what I mean. Of course I'll

do my part no matter what. More—if you'll let me. But my point is, the legal contract of marriage makes things easier all around. The baby will automatically become my dependent. There won't be any hassles with the Air Force in regard to providing all the benefits that go along with the fact that I'm a veteran."

He saw her brows pinch together in dubious consideration at that. He pushed on. "Think about it, Faith. You have your own business. You know how expensive buying your own health care is. If we're married, you'll have coverage not only for the baby forever, but for yourself, as well. During the delivery."

She bit at her lower lip, looking bewildered.

"There's not only the legal and financial considerations," he continued. "I'd love to say that in this day and age, it doesn't matter to a child whether his parents have ever been married or not, but I think we'd both agree that just isn't the case." When he saw the doubt and anxiety lingering on her face, he threw out his trump card. He hadn't wanted to use it, but Faith wasn't going to give him any choice in this.

"We can get a divorce after the baby is

born, if you like," he said. He forced himself not to grimace at the words.

He was desperate for Faith to accept him into her life. If he had to resort to partial measures in order to gain her compliance, he'd take what he could get. His only hope was that if she allowed him in partially, he could eventually coax her into accepting him completely. Faith clearly had doubts about his worthiness as a partner. Given her past with Jesse, he couldn't say he blamed her.

He just needed a chance. An opportunity to prove himself, once and for all.

He slid his hand into his jacket pocket. Her eyes went huge when he opened up the ring box. The lights from the interior of the restaurant glittered in the center diamond brilliant and glowed like a subdued fire in emeralds surrounding the band.

"I hope you like it," he said. "I chose the emeralds to match your eyes."

She looked bowled over.

"Are you really that shocked?" he asked. "I would have thought you were at least partially expecting something like this. It's not like I haven't made it clear I have feelings for you."

He instantly regretted saying that. A panicked look entered her expression.

"Ryan, you're just saying that because of the circumstances. You're under no obligation to do this."

He shook his head and gave a small bark of laughter. "I don't feel obligated, Faith. I *want* to do this."

"For the baby, right?" she asked shakily.

"Right," he said grimly. It wasn't really a lie. He was partially doing this for the baby. The baby was his, after all.

The baby was *theirs.* As in, theirs *together.*

He just needed to prove to Faith that *she* was his, as well. And just as he'd suspected, he thought as he studied her anxious face, it wasn't going to be a simple challenge.

Faith stared at the most beautiful ring she'd ever seen and felt herself spinning. Her heart throbbed so loudly in her ears, she wondered if Ryan could hear it. He wanted her to marry again?

He wanted her to marry *him*?

She stared up at him helplessly, the lovely ring winking in the dim light as if to coax her.

"Ryan… I don't know what to say."

"Think about it, then. You can give me your answer when you're ready." Despite her doubts, a sharp pain of disappointment went through her when he closed the ring box and slipped it back into his pocket. He put his hands on her shoulders and pulled her closer, so that her lower belly was flush against his groin and her breasts pressed against his ribs. "But there's one thing I should make clear. I don't want there to be any doubt how much I want you. I kept my attraction for you buried while you were married to Jesse. I wasn't even aware of its magnitude until Christmas Eve. I'm not going to lie to myself about it anymore. And I'm not going to lie to you."

He bent and covered her mouth with his. He felt her small, surprised gasp, sensed the heat behind her parted lips. Altering the angle of the kiss, he sought with his tongue, relishing her sweetness. Just one taste and he found himself hardening for her, the lash of desire striking sharp, stinging nerve and flesh. He felt her mouth soften beneath him. Triumph soared through him when her tongue began to duel shyly with his. He pulled her closer in his arms, deepening the already ravenous kiss.

His hands settled on her hips. He palmed her hungrily, loving how her curves fit his hands.

He pushed her even closer against his body, groaning quietly when he felt her softness cradle his arousal. He wanted her again, with the strength and heat of a thousand suns. He didn't think he could take much more of standing on the sidelines, ravenous and craving while Faith was just out of his reach.

He lifted his head, nipping at her lips.

"I want to make love to you again. I have every second...of every day...since that first time," he said quietly between gentle, hungry kisses on her mouth. "Tell me that you want that, too."

"I do," she said breathlessly, returning his feverish kisses avidly.

Arousal raged in him at her admission. "Then let's go. Would you like to come to my hotel room? Or would you prefer we go to your house?"

It took him a moment to realize she was no longer participating as eagerly in their kiss. He lifted his head and studied her face. The uncertainty he saw there sliced through his lust like a sharp blade. Perhaps she noticed his disappointment, because her tone sounded apologetic when she spoke.

"Ryan, if you want me to consider your proposal of marriage seriously, I don't think we should cloud the picture by sleeping together."

He pulled her closer next to his body, making sure she knew the profound effect she had on him. "It's kind of hard to be completely rational when I want you so much," he said. "Maybe we could think clearer if we just gave in to it?"

She gave him a suspicious look, and then laughed when she saw his small smile.

"You can't blame a guy for trying," he muttered. He released her with extreme reluctance. She gathered her wrap around her and looked up at him solemnly.

"I want to think this over," she explained. "It's hard to do that when you're…we're…"

"I understand." He sighed.

She bit her lip and stared out at the black lake. "I think I should probably go home. I have a lot to think about," she said.

He ran his hand along her shawl-covered arm.

"I'll be available. If you want to talk about

the idea of marriage, just call me. But while you're thinking things over, I should return to San Francisco. There's a lot I need to do if I intend to move the charter airline business to Michigan."

"Do you still plan to do that? Even if we don't...marry?" she finished awkwardly.

He nodded. "I purchased the Cessna that was for sale at the airport, and I've arranged to rent space there for my planes and an office."

"Really? You've been busy," she said, sounding a little numb.

"I haven't changed my mind about wanting to be near my son or daughter. I don't think I could stand being that far away on a regular basis from my child." *Or from you,* he finished privately. If he said that out loud, she'd run scared. He'd already witnessed how skittish she could become at the idea of them in a romantic relationship. For now his best bet would be to give her the space she needed to feel confident in her decision. He touched her cheek with his fingertips, wishing he could erase the doubt and fear on her face.

"Take your time. I'll be here, whenever you need me," Ryan said.

"Thank you," she whispered, smiling up at him. Something twisted in his gut when he saw tears shining in her eyes.

Two weeks later Faith took off work a little early and stopped by the grocery store. Tonight was a special night. She wanted to make a nice dinner and there were still some last-minute details at the house that needed completing.

At around six that evening she finished making the bed in the guest bedroom, taking extra time to fluff the pillows. Her heart raced with nervous anticipation. She'd already showered and dressed in a manner that she hoped looked nice without seeming like she *tried* to look nice. The steaks she planned to make on the grill were marinating and the green bean, grape and pasta salad was ready to serve.

She ran her hand across the pillowcase, trying to picture Ryan's head resting there. It seemed surreal, but it was going to happen. Tonight. Ryan had already arrived in Holland. He would be at her house at any moment.

For a period of time—it would be *his* house, as well.

A week after the fundraiser ball, following a great deal of soul-searching, she'd called him in California and agreed to marry him. He'd taken another week to tidy up matters with his business and put his condo up for sale. In all that time Faith hadn't seen him. She missed him more than she cared to admit, his absence feeling like a raw ache in her belly, which she continually told herself was a figment of her imagination or quite possibly indigestion from her pregnant state.

She'd made clear her requirements for the marriage, of course. It would be in name only. Ryan could live at her house until the divorce was final—in the spare bedroom. They would remain married until the baby was born, giving their child at least the basics of legitimacy. Faith wouldn't have cared about such a thing; her baby would be loved to the ends of the earth, no matter what legal contract had been observed or not observed at the time of its birth. However she didn't want to deprive her baby of any of the benefits of a "normal" childhood.

Whatever "normal" meant.

She now had an inkling of what Ryan had meant about the social stigma associated with having a child out of wedlock, as much as she wished she hadn't gained knowledge of that particular prejudice. Her parents had been stunned and somewhat stiff when she'd informed them the day after the fundraiser that she was pregnant. When she'd called them back, and informed them that she planned to elope with Ryan—the father of her baby— they'd seemed somewhat mollified.

Faith knew her parents were utterly involved with each other, their friends and their social schedule. She wasn't offended that they'd seemed relieved when she said Ryan and she planned to elope in a small, private ceremony, and that they wouldn't be required to fly from their cozy condominium to Michigan. She routinely made excuses for her parents' lackluster interest in her life, and had long ago accepted the fact that Bob and Myra Blackwell were more interested in each other and their social network than they'd ever been in their only daughter. Faith described them as "deliriously happy in their golden years," for instance, while her friend Jane was known to dub them "self-involved excuses for parents."

In all honesty Faith wasn't much bothered by the idea that her parents couldn't be roused from their routine to attend her wedding. Given the facade of the marriage, she'd prefer not to have too many witnesses to the event.

She stood next to the bed and glanced around Ryan's new bedroom suite, anxious to make sure everything was neat and orderly. Her stomach seemed to leap into her chest cavity when she heard the brisk knock at her front door.

She opened her mouth to greet him when she opened the outer door, but nothing came out. He looked amazing to her. In the two weeks of his absence, his hair had grown a little bit. It now brushed his collar in the back and fell farther forward on his forehead. Along with a slight scruff on his lean jaw and the duffel bag flung casually over his shoulder, he appeared to be exactly what she'd subtly accused him of being in the past—a bad-boy, extremely sexy pilot with the promise of a new adventure gleaming in his eyes. Or maybe the reason her brain immediately leaped to "sex" had to do with the way his dark eyes trailed over her in a preylike perusal, as though he was calmly planning where he was going to take his first bite.

She cleared her throat and forced her ridiculous thoughts to scatter.

"Welcome back," she said breathlessly. "Or should I say, welcome home."

He grinned—a quick, brilliant flash of sex appeal.

"Thanks," he said, stepping into the foyer when she waved her hand and stepped back.

"Did everything go okay with your arrival in Holland?" Faith asked as she led him to his bedroom, her chin twisted over her shoulder. She was having trouble pulling her stare off his rugged male glory and nearly passed the doorway to his room.

"Yeah, all went well. Both planes are snug in their new homes at the airport, and I dropped Scott off at his new apartment," he said, referring to the other pilot for Eagle Air.

"So Scott is all settled?" Faith asked as they hovered outside the room.

"Yeah. He wants to thank you in person for all you've done in helping him. He liked the apartment a lot. I want to thank you, too, Faith, for looking at some places and sending him the apartment photos and the phone numbers for getting utilities connected and everything."

"Mari took care of some things, as well," she reminded him, flipping on the light and leading him into the room.

"I know. We're thankful to both of you. I'm glad Scott decided to make the move with me. He's too good of a pilot to lose. Besides, he's as much of a workhorse as I am," Ryan said distractedly, his gaze moving around the bedroom and finally landing on Faith.

"I can't believe you did all this," he said, sounding stunned.

"You...you like it, don't you?" Faith asked, referring to the newly refurbished bedroom.

"I can't believe you did all this," he repeated, looking almost grim. He plopped his large duffel bag on the bed and came toward her. "You shouldn't have, Faith," he admonished, looking all around the room again and then back at her. "I would have been happy sleeping on the couch. You didn't have to redecorate a whole room."

"It's just new bedding and curtains."

"And new lamps, and rugs...and was that painting there before?" he asked, referring to the framed Lake Michigan landscape.

"No," she admitted, feeling uncomfortable under his blazing stare.

He muttered something under his breath and stepped closer. Her breath stuck in her lungs when he took her into his arms, making the action seem as natural as climbing into the pilot's seat of an F-16.

"You shouldn't have spent all that time and money on me," he said quietly, his voice resonating above her forehead. She looked up slowly. It overwhelmed her a little—a lot—to feel his rock-hard body next to hers, to see his bold-featured, much-missed visage so close. "I'll pay you back for everything you purchased."

"No, that's not necessary. I wanted to make it a nice place for you," she said, her voice just above a whisper, her eyes caught in his steady stare.

"I missed you while I was gone," he said.

"I... I missed you, too," she admitted shakily. She ducked her head when he lowered his. She was sorely tempted to lift it again, to accept his kiss—to glory in it. Because there was little doubt, given the glint in his eyes and the rigid expression of his features, kissing her had been *precisely* what Ryan was about to do. She couldn't allow their arrangement to derail from her planned course within three minutes of his arrival at the house.

"Why don't you get unpacked, and I'll go and get us some lemonade in the kitchen," Faith said, backing out of his arms. Her false cheeriness stood in stark contrast to Ryan's slanted brows and slightly irritated expression.

He entered the kitchen several minutes later. She glanced sideways at him as he bent to greet an ecstatic Topsy and ruffle the puppy's coat.

"Look at you. You've grown, haven't you, little girl?" he murmured, grinning.

It was an unusually warm spring day and he wore a short-sleeved white T-shirt and a pair of jeans. The shirt displayed his muscular arms ideally. Faith paused in the action of garnishing their drinks with lime slices.

"I didn't know you had a tattoo," she said, eyeing the only partially revealed depiction of what appeared to be a bird with outstretched wings etched on steely biceps just beneath a white sleeve.

He stood, a darkly amused look on his

face. "You haven't given me the opportunity to show it to you yet."

She blushed and busied herself putting away the ice-cube container. It was true what he'd said—they'd been so wild with lust on Christmas Eve, they hadn't really had the opportunity for the niceties.

Like fully undressing, for instance.

What he'd said was also just a bit too *intimate*, given the comfortable, safe parameters she was trying to immediately establish in regard to their cohabitation.

"Ryan," she began with forced calmness, handing him his lemonade, "if we're going to make this work, we have to…respect each other's boundaries."

His dark brows lifted at her schoolmarm tone of voice. "I wasn't trying to be disrespectful. I was just stating the truth," he said, taking a sip of lemonade. She couldn't help but grin when he made a sound of appreciation, then swallowed the contents of the glass in three large swigs.

"Sorry," he said a moment later. "I was helping Scott move around some of his furniture, and it's hot out today. I was thirstier than I thought, and it tasted great."

"It's nice out in the shade on the back terrace. Do you want to sit out there?" Faith asked, holding up the pitcher to refill his glass. She was a little alarmed by his level of familiarity—not to mention the heat of his stare. She thought it would be advisable to take the opportunity to rehash the "rules" of their arrangement before things slipped into foolish chaos.

He agreed about going to the terrace, and the three of them—Topsy, Ryan and Faith—retired to the back terrace.

"Everything's blooming," Ryan said as he sat down in a deck chair and surveyed the backyard. "Including you."

Faith paused in the action of settling in the chair next to him. Her glance dropped to her belly. It was definitely protruding a little next to the fabric of the cotton shorts she wore. She'd originally thought the embroidered peasant blouse she wore to be a modest, yet feminine choice for Ryan's arrival. Suddenly she wondered if instead of looking prim, she didn't more resemble the busty serving wench on the side of a beer bottle.

She froze, her lemonade glass trembling in her hand, when he leaned over on his hip and matter-of-factly placed his hand on her belly. After a second she inhaled sharply, stunned by the weight of his hand on her rising abdomen.

"Have you really been feeling okay?" Ryan asked, his voice sounding husky and nearer than she expected.

She nodded, keeping her gaze aimed straight ahead. He'd called every few days during his absence and always asked her about her health.

"I talked to Mari yesterday. She told me that you were showing—a little tiny bit, anyway," he said, shifting his hand upward. Prickles of pleasure went through her. Her breasts were growing so full that in her partially reclining position, his hand almost cradled them. "She said you two found a dress. For the wedding."

"We did," Faith said, trying to sound normal. She took a swig of her lemonade, feeling ridiculous doing something so mundane while Ryan touched her so intimately. She knew she should tell him to stop touching her, but she couldn't help but feel it would draw attention to the significance of the contact...

...the *impact* it was having on her.

"I needed something new anyway. I've gone up a size, with the baby," she explained, hoping he didn't think she'd gone shopping like a breathless bride for her dream wedding dress. "Mari and I had a nice time, shopping together for it in downtown Holland. We went to lunch afterward." She risked a sideways glance. His gaze was glued to her face, but his hand lowered over her belly, as if he were tracing the slight convexness. He was just eager to feel his growing child, that's all. She tried like crazy to ignore the fireworks of sensation going off in her body as his hand reached the lower curve, his pinky resting at the top of her pelvis. A heavy, pleasant ache expanded at her core.

Focus, she told herself.

"Your sister is such a wonderful person. I can't wait to meet Marc," Faith said in a pressured fashion, desperate to turn her attention away from Ryan's stroking hand. "Are you close to Marc?" she asked in an odd, high-pitched voice as she blindly watched Topsy sink her sharp little teeth into a chew toy.

His deck chair squeaked next to her, and Faith realized he'd leaned closer. His hand moved yet again, the slight bump in her belly curving into his palm.

"We used to be best friends when we were kids," Ryan murmured, sounding distracted. Faith nervously took a sip of lemonade as his hand slid up her abdomen. This time he went farther, the ridge of his forefinger grazing her lower breasts. "Before the accident his father caused, that is," he added, moving his hand in a slight sawing motion, stimulating the sensitive skin of her ribs.

Faith stifled a choking sound. Her nipples drew tight against the clinging fabric of her bra.

"After the accident, Marc and I had a falling out," Ryan continued quietly. Faith struggled to recall the topic. His hand lowered again, this time detailing the side of her abdomen, making it very difficult for her to breathe. "A pretty severe falling out, actually. It came to blows during the lawsuit hearings, I remember."

"You two fought?" Faith asked, startled. She found herself examining his dark head and profile. He stared fixedly at his hand on her stomach. He nodded.

"Yeah. It almost came to blows again a few

years ago when Mari got involved with him after all this time. They were teenage sweethearts, you know."

"No. I didn't."

"Then the accident happened. And the lawsuits," Ryan said so grimly that she temporarily forgot her discomfort—and arousal—at his possessive caress. Compassion for him filled her. She touched a crisp, short sideburn and he tilted his head, spearing her with his stare.

"It must have been so hard for you all—that accident, the losses…everything that came after it."

He said nothing, but his dark eyes spoke to her, nonetheless.

"Will it be difficult for you? To have Mari and Marc stand up for us when we get…married on Sunday?" she asked, fumbling and blushing at the mention of what they would be doing in three days time.

"No. It'll be fine," he said.

It suddenly struck her that they were touching each other very intimately and speaking in hushed tones. She'd called him out here to clarify the safe boundaries of their arrangement, and instead, Ryan's touch had turned her into a quivering, aroused bundle of nerves.

She dropped her hand and looked away. Slowly, Ryan removed his hand. She could almost feel his disappointment.

Or was it disapproval?

"So we're all set? For the wedding?" he said, the location of his voice informing her that he'd leaned back in his chair.

"Yes. Father Mike will meet all of us at the orchard," she said, trying to sound matter-of-fact, even though she was breathless and she could still feel the imprint of his hand on her abdomen. "It was a wonderful idea that you had, having the ceremony at the McKinley Farm and Orchard. The trees will be in full bloom. It'll be beautiful."

"Marc and Mari actually suggested it. They introduced me to it—and the Cherry Pie Café—last year. The McKinleys are nice people."

Faith smiled. She knew the orchard owners, Nathan and Clarisse McKinley, and had eaten several times at their delicious, lakeside restaurant on the grounds. It'd never occurred to her before how perfect the location would be for a spring wedding.

Not that this was a real wedding or anything, she quickly reminded herself.

Ryan checked his watch. He cursed quietly and sat up with a start.

"What's wrong?" Faith asked.

"I have to go. I have a flight. I'm taking a couple DuBois Enterprises executives from Chicago to New York."

"Oh," Faith said, taken aback. "I hadn't realized you'd start working so soon."

He grimaced slightly as he glanced at her and placed his long legs on either side of the lounge chair in preparation to stand. "You don't mind, do you? I'll be back by the time you wake up tomorrow. I was lucky to get a contract with DuBois. It's going to keep me busy. *Extremely* busy. I should be able to buy another plane soon, with as much work as Deidre and Nick are willing to send my way. I want to build a lucrative business, Faith. For the baby. For the future," he added, his dark eyes moving over her face.

"Of course," she said, feeling embarrassed, all thoughts of her warm welcome dinner for him fizzling to mist. Had she sounded whiny because he was leaving so soon after his arrival? She hadn't meant to. She admired him for working so hard to build up his company. "I'll go in with you and give you the key to the front door."

"Thanks." He touched her cheek and gently tucked a curl behind her ear. Faith tried to ignore the tendril of pleasure that coiled down her neck at his touch, just like she tried to ignore the fact that she was disappointed he was leaving.

After Ryan had left for the airport, she wondered why the house felt so empty. It made no sense whatsoever. She'd lived alone there for over a year, and never felt lonely. Now Ryan had blown through her front door and flown off after just an hour, and the house already felt empty in his absence.

It worried her, how easily she could get used to his presence; how much she could come to count on it.

It meant she'd be all that much more disappointed when he was gone. How much more proof did she need than tonight, that a man like Ryan wasn't meant to stay in one place for long?

No. That wasn't going to happen, she told herself firmly as she started down the hallway. She wasn't going to become dependent on his being there. Hadn't she been happy and satisfied for almost her entire adult life by calling her own shots?

So if she was so confident that she didn't need Ryan Itani one way or another, why did she pause outside his opened bedroom door? She hesitated, and then entered slowly. She stood at the mirrored chest of drawers and ran her fingers over a leather box, a bottle of his cologne and a handsome gold watch, dressier than the black casual one she'd seen on his wrist before he'd left.

He might be in his plane at this moment, preparing to fly away from Holland. But his things were here, hallmarks of his presence, reminders that even if it *was* temporary, for a period of time, this was Ryan's home.

She tried to ignore the feeling of satisfaction that tore through her at the thought, but it was just as hard to banish as her other feelings were when it came to Ryan.

She saved the dinner she'd made, in case Ryan wanted it tomorrow. By the time she made herself a grilled cheese sandwich and ate, it was getting late. She had a seven o'clock appointment at the office, so decided to retire early. She made sure some fresh towels were laid out for Ryan in his bathroom—he might want to shower when he got home early in the morning.

Now that she was pregnant, sleep came almost immediately the second her cheek hit the pillow. It took a little longer tonight, as thoughts and worries about Ryan moving in and their upcoming marriage whirled around her consciousness. Still, she was fast asleep by the time her bedside clock dial turned to ten o'clock.

She awoke with a start in the middle of the night. She just lay there, her heart racing, trying to figure out what had startled her. There hadn't been a noise, had there? It took her panicked brain several seconds to recall that it was probably Ryan returning home from his flight. She glanced at her clock. It read 4:35 a.m. She heard a tiny squeak from the hallway floor, as if someone was walking down it with caution.

It was *Ryan out there, wasn't it?* she thought anxiously.

She rose and scurried for her robe, donning it over the thigh-length nightshirt she wore. She gave a sigh of relief when she saw the light on in the kitchen in the distance and heard the sound of the refrigerator door open. Surely a burglar wouldn't make himself a late-night snack. Even knowing it was Ryan, however, anticipation coiled in her belly as she walked around the corner into the kitchen.

He stood next to the refrigerator, the door open.

"Hi," Faith said.

He peered around the door. The refrigerator swung closed. "I'm sorry," he said quietly. "I didn't mean to wake you. Was I too loud?"

Faith shook her head, staring. He was only wearing a pair of dark blue pajama bottoms. And by all things that were holy, she'd never seen a more beautiful man in her life.

She gaped at the vision before her of rippling, hard muscle covered by golden skin. She now could see that the tattoo on bulging, powerful-looking biceps was the Air Force logo that had been artfully depicted by the illustrator as transforming into a real eagle taking flight.

She swallowed with difficulty. Her throat had gone completely dry.

"Faith?" Ryan asked, looking a little worried.

"No, no. You weren't loud at all. I'm just used to living alone. I must have a sixth sense, about someone being in the house," she said, her gaze darting everywhere around the room, trying to avoid gawking at the awesome sight of his half-naked body. She cleared her throat and told herself to get a grip. "Would you like me to make you something to eat?"

"No. I was just going to make some toast or something, if that's okay. I haven't eaten since we left New York this morning."

Her expression collapsed in compassion. "You must be starved." She swept toward the refrigerator. He took a step back. "Just sit down over there in the breakfast nook, and I'll get something for you."

"Faith—"

"How about a cheese omelet and toast?" she asked, already grabbing the eggs. She paused, looking up at him when he put a hand on her forearm, halting her.

"I don't want you to cook for me. It's four-thirty in the morning. You should go back to bed."

She shrugged. "I'm up now. I have to be at the office at seven, anyway." His furrowed brow smoothed slightly when she gave him a smile of reassurance. "Will it help any if I eat with you?"

He shook his head and looked skyward, as though looking for patience in dealing with her. "Does it make any difference what I say?" he asked dryly.

She shook her head matter-of-factly. "Why don't you sit down in the breakfast nook? I'll bring you some juice."

"I don't want you to wait on me," he grumbled. He released her arm and reached into the refrigerator himself. "I'll pour the juice and make the toast."

"Deal. How was your flight?" she asked him a moment later as she whipped the eggs in a bowl and Ryan plugged in the toaster.

"Pretty uneventful. Just the way I like them." He gave her a backward glance. Her cheeks heated as she returned her attention to the eggs. He'd caught her staring at the way his back muscles rippled when he moved.

"Faith?"

"Yes?" she asked, looking around and hoping he didn't notice her pink cheeks.

He stepped toward her. His naked torso was like a miracle of taut ridges, valleys and dense, swelling muscle. His skin was beautiful—smooth and dark-honey colored. A smattering of dark hair grew on his chest, but not thickly. A thin, tempting trail of it led from his taut bellybutton and disappeared beneath the low-riding cotton pants.

She felt as if her lungs had failed her as he drew nearer.

"When I was looking in the refrigerator before you came in, I noticed—" He halted, looking a little uncomfortable. "Were you planning on making dinner? Last night?"

He definitely had to notice her blush now.

"Oh...yes. But it wasn't a big deal. I just thought I'd throw something on the grill, you know. Just a little welcome dinner..."

She faded off, feeling scored by his stare. She turned around and began beating the eggs again, pausing when she felt Ryan put his hands on her shoulders. He applied a slight pressure. Reluctantly she set the whisk in the bowl and turned to face him. He stood close enough that a bulging pectoral muscle was less than a foot away from her face. He pushed back her unbound hair from her cheek, smoothing it over her shoulder. Her neck tingled with pleasure. His fingertips brushed against the shell of her ear, and her shivering amplified.

"I'm sorry I ruined the evening," he said quietly.

"You didn't ruin anything," she insisted, looking up to reassure him. "You had a job. It wasn't a big deal."

His face looked somber as he studied her. He cradled her jaw with his hand. She felt so small in comparison to him. So feminine standing there next to his large, hard male body. She realized she was holding her breath.

"It *was* a big deal." She stared at him, mesmerized. His nostrils flared slightly and his face drew nearer. "I'll make it up to you, I promise."

"There's nothing to make up. It was nothing," she said, the words popping out of her with her expelled breath.

"I disagree," he murmured. His lips moved now just inches from her own. He stepped forward with his right foot, so that his inner thigh touched the outside of her hip. He leaned into her and she was wedged between Ryan and the counter. "It was sweet of you. *You're* incredibly sweet, Faith."

His hands tightened around her waist. He

paused, his face just inches from her own. She met his stare, wide-eyed, and saw he was watching her like a hawk. Her lips parted.

He swooped down, seizing her mouth with his own.

Chapter Nine

His mouth moved over hers, a sensual drug that left her consciousness hazed by pleasure. He pressed closer, nudging her middle. Her eyes popped open, even though she kept avidly participating in the kiss. He wasn't wearing anything beneath the thin fabric of the pajama bottoms.

His obvious arousal made something squeeze tight deep inside her, made her recall all too well how he'd filled her on Christmas Eve, how he'd pulsed high and hard and alive deep inside her. Desire sluiced through her, so sharp she cried out softly into his hot, marauding mouth.

She touched his back with her hands, relishing the sensation of smooth skin gloving muscle and bone so tightly. Her fingertips moved eagerly, detailing the line of his spine. Her palms swept over the expanse of his back, pushing him closer.

He came up for air, making a hissing sound.

"I know you think we shouldn't give in to this, Faith, but for the life of me, how can I forget what you felt like that night?" he whispered roughly next to her lips. "You were so small..." He plucked at her upturned lips. "So sweet. I can't sleep at night, remembering how good it felt," he muttered as he reined feverish kisses on her lips, her cheek, her ear. His hands moved at her waist, stroking her back, lowering to cup her hips possessively. He brought her closer, shifting his pelvis, rubbing their flesh together, stoking the fire.

Faith found herself sinking into heat.

"Please let me make love to you again," he said hoarsely, covering her ear with his mouth. The suction that came from his kiss caused prickles of excitement to reverberate down her spine. "I've thought about it since Christmas. How could something that feels this good be wrong?" His hand rose over her ribs, finding a breast. He covered her, nestling her flesh in his palm. She whimpered as he began to knead her gently. Her nipple grew hard against him. He gave a low growl of male approval. His body tensed and hardened next to hers.

She gasped in pleasure.

"You think so, too," he rasped.

"Yes," she whispered, her mouth seeking out his. "Yes," she breathed next to his lips before she pushed his head down to hers. They fastened together in another ravenous kiss. Sensual pleasure suffused every pore in her being. She said nothing when she felt him lift her off her feet. He strode out of the kitchen and through the living room, his stare scorching her. The bedroom was shadowed and dim, the only source of light the one in the distant kitchen and a glowing bedside clock.

He laid her on the bed and came down over her, immediately fusing their mouths again. His body covered hers, with plenty to spare. He felt so hard, so wonderful. Her mind went blank. Only pleasure existed…and Ryan.

His hands moved over her, conferring delight and heat wherever he touched. Faith was far from passive, however, touching him back just as heatedly, relishing the opportunity to feel what she'd barely allowed herself to look at earlier. His hands found their way to the belt of her robe, loosening it, and then moved to her thighs. He raised the fabric of her nightshirt to her waist, pausing to caress and enliven her tingling nerves with every stroke.

"So soft," he rasped, breaking their kiss. He lowered his head. She made a choking sound at the sensation of his mouth pressing between her rib cage. His lips nibbled at her tenderly, making her shiver. He tasted her, his tongue leaving damp spots on her pebbling skin. He pushed up her nightshirt. She gasped at the sensation of his mouth on her breast, moaning as he drew on her. Pleasure tore through her body. Her breasts had never felt so sensitive. He continued to use his mouth and tongue on one nipple, and used his fingertips to gently manipulate the other.

"Ryan," she said helplessly.

"I've never tasted anything as good you," he muttered thickly. He rose over her, his erection between her thighs. Faith's eyes sprang wide at the sensation. She twisted her head on the pillow. Her cheek brushed against the soft fabric of the pillowcase...

...the same pillowcase she'd just put on

last evening. In Ryan's bedroom. The room where he was going to live while they shared a marriage of convenience for the benefit of their child.

She cried out in distress, moving her chin when Ryan bent again to ravish her mouth. He paused, his lips just inches from her averted jaw. She clamped her eyes shut when she felt a whole new type of tension enter his sleek muscles.

"We can't," she said shakily. "This isn't how this was supposed to go, Ryan."

"I thought things were going pretty damn great," he said grimly.

"Ryan…"

He cursed under his breath and rolled off her. She came up on her elbows, staring at his shadowed figure anxiously.

"I'm sorry," she said. "I shouldn't have agreed to this. This whole moving in together…the marriage idea. It was a mistake."

He lowered his arm. "No. You weren't at fault," he said, his voice hard. She heard him inhale slowly. When he resumed speaking, he sounded calmer. "It was my fault. I'm to blame. I agreed to respect your boundaries under this arrangement. I didn't."

"I was hardly complaining," she said miserably, moving to the side of the bed. He caught her hand and she paused.

"It won't happen again. Not unless you change your mind."

Her mouth fell open. Guilt surged through her. He was making it sound like he'd taken advantage of her, when goodness knows she'd been every bit as eager for him as he was her.

Not unless you change your mind.

She reluctantly pulled her hand from his and stood at the side of the bed.

The problem was, Faith couldn't trust herself. She couldn't tell Ryan that what she *wanted* was him.

What she *didn't* want was all the heartache she might receive if she opened herself up to him too far.

All was quiet in his bedroom when she crept out of the house on Friday morning. When she returned home that night, a heavy pregnancy-exhaustion weighting her muscles, she found a note in the kitchen from Ryan. It said he'd taken a flight to San Francisco, and that he'd just spend the night in his still-unsold condo before returning on Saturday.

Check the fridge, she read the last line few lines of his note. *A peace offering. I'm sorry about last night. I'm not sure how it is I'm always screwing things up when all I really want is to get it right with you.*

Tears burned her eyelids. She opened the refrigerator.

The first thing she saw was a luscious-looking dessert nestled in a paper cup with thick shavings of white chocolate nestled in frosting. She recognized it as her favorite guilty pleasure from the bakery downtown—a brownie with white chocolate chunks and Macadamia nuts. She pictured a smiling Georgiana at the bakery telling Ryan about Faith's preferred dessert.

Beneath the confection was a plastic-covered plate. She grabbed it and the brownie and set them on the counter. When she peeled back the plastic on the plate, she saw that he'd grilled the steak she'd pre-pared for his thwarted welcome dinner. He'd placed a helping of her green bean, grape and pasta salad next to it.

She stared blankly at the meal he'd made for a full minute, her throat feeling tight. She'd treated him unfairly last night. Her guilt mounted over the fact that he kept apologizing for a sin she'd participated in every bit as enthusiastically as he had. There was a singular, powerful attraction between them. Ryan was just a man; one who was undoubtedly unused to having his sexual advances denied.

Faith knew firsthand how difficult it was to deny him.

How fair was it for her to agree to this arrangement between them, knowing full well that she was making him uncomfortable?

Miserable?

What if, even now, he was finding the gratification she'd denied him last night in the arms of another woman?

"Don't be stupid," she snapped at herself out loud. She picked up the plate and cupcake and set them on the breakfast nook table.

She'd drive herself absolutely mad by having thoughts like that every time Ryan took off in a plane.

She arose the next morning to a pristine, sunny spring day. As she was preparing some breakfast, she heard her cell phone ringing. She answered it when she saw it was Mari calling.

"Good morning," she greeted, setting her steaming bowl of oatmeal on the table.

"Good morning!" Mari returned cheerfully. "How are you feeling?"

"Wonderful," Faith said honestly. "I'm always energized in the mornings."

"And wiped out by two o'clock, right?" Mari said knowingly. "The fatigue is supposed to go away for a lot of women during the second trimester and come back for the last, but I know for me, I'm affected the whole time."

"Unfortunately, I think we might have that in common," Faith said dryly, touching her abdomen. "I'm not complaining, though. Luckily, I can go into my office if it gets too bad and close my eyes for fifteen minutes."

"Those catnaps make a world of difference. I just wanted to tell you that Marc and I are spending the night with Brigit tonight in Harbor Town. I can drive over this afternoon if there are any last-minute details you'd like me to see to for the wedding. Ryan called last night, and said he would be in San Francisco until later today. He thought you might need some help."

Warmth rushed through her at the mention

of Ryan's concern for her. "Oh, no. I'm fine. There really isn't much to plan, it's going to be such a simple ceremony. Ryan has gotten the license, and you helped me with the dress and Ryan's ring. Clarisse is going to make the four of us a nice lunch on the terrace after the ceremony. I hear the weather is supposed to be wonderful. Everything is all taken care of."

"So you don't have any errands you need run today?"

"No, I'm actually seeing some patients at the office this morning, I got so backed up this week. But I really appreciate you asking, Mari," she said sincerely.

"Well, call me if you change your mind. Oh... I spoke with Deidre on the phone earlier. She wants me to tell you congratulations. Ryan told her and Nick about you and the baby and his plans to headquarter Eagle Air out of Michigan. Nick thinks it's a good thing, as so many DuBois employees have to regularly go coast-to-coast, and Ryan will be more centrally located."

"Tell Deidre thank you. And as for Eagle Air, I'm happy to hear it's going to work for everybody."

They reaffirmed the time they would meet at the orchard tomorrow and said goodbye.

As Mari had predicted, Faith was exhausted by the time she returned home at a little past three that afternoon. She fed the cats and let Topsy into the yard. After she let the puppy back inside, she kicked off her pumps and flopped down on the couch in the living room. The sun shone through the large picture window next to the couch, warming her. After a minute Topsy came up to the couch, whining plaintively.

"Hi you," Faith murmured, leaning down to scoop up the fluffy puppy in her arms. She curled on her left side, Topsy snuggling between her body and the back of the couch. She closed her eyes and drifted into a contented sleep.

Ryan pulled into the driveway, his eyes feeling gritty with fatigue. He hadn't slept well last night, tossing and turning, recalling in vivid detail what had occurred with Faith the night before, wishing it hadn't happened…

…wanting like hell for it to happen again. He had to rise early to fly a DuBois exec-

utive from San Francisco to Houston. He'd
been forced to wait two hours before being
cleared for takeoff in Houston, chomping at
the bit the whole time for his return to Michigan.

To Faith.

The interior of the house was bright and
warm when he entered. "Faith?" he called,
his voice trailing off at the utter silence of the
house. He walked out of the foyer and immediately saw her curled up on the couch. He
approached her cautiously, a smile tugging at
his mouth when he noticed Topsy tucked next
to her body, both of them taking the even,
shallow breaths of sleep.

He sat down at the end of the couch, careful that his movements wouldn't wake her.
He sank into the cushion with a restrained
sigh, his tired muscles relaxing at last. Faith
hadn't changed since she'd returned home
from the office. He'd noticed that she tended
to only wear the tailored, knee-length skirts
for work. Her bare legs looked smooth, pale
and shapely next to the taupe fabric of the
couch. The bottoms of her feet looked feminine and pink and…extremely touchable.

He'd promised not to touch her, though,

he recalled with a stab of grim disappointment. Instead he grabbed the decorative pillow wedged behind his back and the couch and wrapped his arms around it. It was nowhere near as warm as Faith, or as soft, or as shapely.

But it'd have to do.

Faith felt Topsy's warm body moving and shifted, stretching her legs. Her feet were chilly. She sunk almost immediately back into sleep.

When she finally pried open her eyelids a while later, the light outside the window had dimmed. It was early evening. Her intended catnap had turned into a two-hour deep sleep. She felt so warm and cozy, she was tempted to get up and go back to her bed.

She lifted her head off the pillow and started. She blinked, bringing her sleepy eyes into focus, assuring herself she saw what she *thought* she was seeing. Ryan came into clearer view. He sat at the end of the couch, his long, jean-covered legs sprawled before him. Topsy had abandoned her only to relocate next to him. The puppy snuggled against his hip, her nose pressed next to his thigh.

Faith's feet were in his lap, his hand draped over her toes in a relaxed grip. Her eyes widened when she saw—and felt—just how intimately her feet were pressed against the fly of his jeans.

She started to extricate her feet from the compromising position, but paused when Ryan's head moved on the back of the couch. She froze. She vaguely recalled stretching her feet earlier and finding a warm crevice in which to snuggle them.

To her rising horror, she saw Ryan open his eyes.

For a few tense seconds they just stared at each other, unmoving. His heat seemed to amplify beneath her, resonating into her feet. His hand tightened as if convulsively over her toes, then loosened.

Faith jerked her feet out of his lap.

"I'm sorry," he muttered, his voice sounding sleep-roughened and sexy. He blinked, as if clearing his vision. "I drifted off when I got home. Didn't sleep well last night."

"Neither did I," Faith said, smoothing her skirt over her thighs. She swung her feet to the floor and sat up, avoiding his gaze. "How long... I mean...when did you get home?"

she asked awkwardly, running her fingers through her hair.

"About an hour ago, I think."

Topsy made a sound between a grunt and a whine. Faith turned. Topsy was blinking sleepily. Ryan was watching her face with a narrow-eyed stare.

"I didn't…" He glanced down toward his lap, clearly uncomfortable. "It was… Your feet were just *there* when I woke up."

"I know," she said, standing, suddenly wishing she were anywhere but there. "I know you didn't do it. I think I did. Sleeping…feet cold," she mumbled stupidly before she grabbed her pumps and rushed out of the living room to the safety of her bedroom.

She felt so discombobulated by the experience, so vulnerable, that she closed her bedroom door and drew a hot bath. She took her time bathing, trying to piece together her discordant feelings about Ryan…her attraction to him, her uncontrollable desire…her fear of getting hurt.

An hour later she stood at the mirror in her bathroom, brushing her hair. A soft knock came at her door. She glanced around, her eyes going wide and her heartbeat escalating. She stood there for several seconds, undecided about whether or not she should answer. If she remained quiet, Ryan might assume she was sleeping and go away.

She grabbed her robe and hurriedly shoved her arms into the sleeves, then opened the door. He stood in the dim hallway, still dressed as he had been when they'd awakened on the couch. He looked at her from below a lowered brow.

"I got you a salad from the deli. It's in the fridge," he said quietly.

"Oh, thank you. But I'm not very hungry."

"You should eat."

"Maybe later," she said, her voice barely above a whisper.

He nodded, his gaze flickering over her. "I think I'll go for a jog and try to get to bed early. Big day tomorrow."

She attempted a smile and nodded. Awkwardness flooded her. They were getting married tomorrow, and here they stood, talking to each other like acquaintances through a crack in the door.

"We're still leaving at eleven tomorrow, right?" he asked.

"Yes."

Did he exhale, as if relieved? Had he been thinking she'd changed her mind about tomorrow?

"Well, good night, then," he said.

"Good night. Ryan?" she called impulsively when he turned to walk away. He paused, looking back at her.

"Thank you for making dinner for me last night. And the brownie was delicious."

He smiled. "You made the dinner. I just cooked it."

"Well, thank you anyway," she said emphatically.

He nodded once, his expression tight, his gaze searching. He turned. Faith opened her mouth to halt him again, but uncertainty tightened her throat, silencing her.

The next day dawned even more brilliant than its predecessor. Faith peered out her bedroom window as soon as she arose. The leaves of the oak tree in the side yard had completely unfurled, looking brilliantly green against the backdrop of a cloudless, periwinkle-blue sky. A soft, mild breeze wafted through the window screen.

When she opened her bedroom door, she paused on the threshold. She could hear the muted sound of Ryan moving around in the kitchen. A ridiculous thought occurred to her that she should go back in her room and close the door.

It's unlucky for the groom to see the bride before the wedding.

Where in the world had *that* come from? Faith wondered in amused puzzlement. It wasn't as if they were a real bride and groom, after all.

She peered into the kitchen cautiously, breathing a sigh of relief when she saw that Ryan wore a gray cotton T-shirt along with his pajama bottoms.

"Good morning," she said, feeling shy for some stupid reason.

He looked around, holding a pan lid in his hand.

"Good morning. I made oatmeal. Hungry?"

"I'm starving," she admitted, entering the kitchen and opening the refrigerator. She pulled out a carton of orange juice and poured it into two glasses.

"You never ate your salad last night," he

said. "No wonder you're starved. Were you nauseated? Because of the baby?"

"No. I think that's mostly passed, thank goodness." She returned the carton to the refrigerator and pulled out some English muffins. "I think I might have just been a little… keyed up."

"Nervous, you mean?"

She paused in the action of forking apart a muffin. Ryan leaned next to the counter. It didn't matter that he'd covered his museum-worthy torso with a T-shirt. He still looked roll-out-of-bed delicious.

"Yes," she admitted, dropping her gaze. "Aren't you? A little?" She looked at his face again when he didn't immediately answer.

"I thought you were going to tell me last night that you didn't want to go through with it," he said starkly.

"Oh…well, I was sort of having doubts last night. It's kind of an unusual situation, isn't it?" she asked, turning to put the muffins in the toaster.

"It's for the best. We have the baby to think about."

"I know."

A strained silence ensued.

"Do you feel any different this morning?" he asked.

She looked out the window on to the brilliant spring day. She gave him a small, sheepish smile.

"This morning I'm feeling like...it's an awfully pretty day for a wedding."

His face remained sober for a stretched moment.

Then he smiled the sort of smile a woman remembers for a long, long time.

At ten forty-five that morning, Faith was cursing herself for not asking Mari or Jane or *anyone* to help her get ready. Yes, she knew very well that this was a marriage of convenience, so why in the world had she let Mari talk her into buying the highly romantic silk, strapless, vintage-inspired gown? She started to work up a sweat as she tried to zip it herself, and had to force herself to pause and take some calming breaths.

Her face looked anxious in the reflection of the bathroom mirror. Her heart pounded in her ears. She hadn't been anywhere near this nervous for her wedding to Jesse.

If you don't want to do it, don't, a voice in her head said firmly.

It was as if reminding herself that she had a choice helped to stabilize her faltering resolution. She was doing this for one reason—a *good* reason. The baby. It had nothing to do with how she felt about Ryan, or how he felt about her…or even how he *didn't* feel about her.

Surely she wasn't so selfish as to deny her child the most secure future she could possibly grant it?

She twisted the dress sufficiently to zip it and slid it back into place. She examined herself in the mirror. Maybe Mari's advice had been perfect, after all. The vintage ivory color worked well with her skin tone. She wore her hair down and curled loosely. It spilled around her bare shoulders. She had a wrap, but thanks to the ideal spring day with temperatures in the mid-seventies, she wouldn't need it. The intricate ruched detail around the bodice did a nice job of disguising her expanding breasts. The thing she loved most about the dress, however, was the flowing, light skirt. It made her feel airy and feminine and…

…very much like a bride.

She felt every bit as jittery as a bride on her wedding day when she left her bedroom a moment later and walked into the living room. Ryan was waiting for her, his hands folded behind his back and staring out the front picture window on to the bright spring day.

He turned. She froze.

He wore his Air Force dress uniform, and he looked…amazing. The dark blue coat and trousers were perfectly tailored to his tall form. A matching bow tie, silver trimmed shoulder boards and sleeve braid added to his immaculate, elegant, yet utterly masculine appearance.

She smiled.

"I had no idea you were going to wear your uniform."

"I hope it's okay."

"You look…fantastic."

"You look like something out of a dream."

Faith blinked. He'd sounded so quiet, so matter-of-fact, it took her a moment to absorb his compliment. She blushed.

"Thank you."

"Just a second," he said, walking toward

the kitchen. When he returned, he held a gorgeous bouquet of white roses, pale orchids and sprays of apple and cherry blossoms. "Every bride is supposed to have flowers."

She accepted the bouquet. "Oh, thank you," she said feelingly. "It's gorgeous. When did you ever have time to get it?"

"I picked it up this morning while you were in the shower. After I got my haircut," he said.

"It's almost military short again."

"We're not allowed to wear a dress uniform without a regulation haircut. Even as veterans," he said, returning her smile. "Well? Are you ready to go?"

Something new had joined her anxiety when she'd seen Ryan standing there in his dress uniform, so handsome, tall and proud. A fullness unlike anything she'd ever experienced in her life filled her chest cavity, making her feel breathless with anticipation, excited and thrilled to be alive.

"Are you ready?" he asked quietly.

Faith nodded, unable to pull her gaze off him. He touched the back of her waist and guided her out the door.

Chapter Ten

Faith gasped in pleasure when Ryan turned down the entrance drive to the McKinley Orchards. The lane was lined with brilliantly pink redbud trees in full blossom.

"Oh, look. I've never seen anything so pretty in my life," she said a few minutes later when Ryan opened the car door for her and she alighted. The garden and landscape blazed so bright with spring color, it was almost blinding to the eyes. Brilliant tulips lined the path to the café, but beyond their tame, orderly border, Clarisse and Nathan had let nature do the gardening. Amaryllis, begonia, bluebell and grape hyacinth waved in the gentle breeze. In the distance stood the groves of blooming fruit trees—fuchsia peach blossoms, snow-white apple and pear, lavender plum and pink cherry. The smooth blue sky and the ruffled, sparkling lake provided a soothing backdrop to the vibrant palette of color.

She glanced at Ryan and they shared a smile.

Several people were walking to greet them along the stone-paved path that led to the café. Mari looked like part of the landscape in a magenta-colored dress with her hair spilling around her shoulders. The tall, arrestingly handsome man with the golden-brown hair and tawny skin who walked by her side must be Marc Kavanaugh. She recognized the sunburned, white-haired, thin man with a camera strapped around his neck as Nathan McKinley, the orchard owner. The man who brought up the rear of the party must be Father Mike.

"Could you possibly have picked a more perfect day for this?" Mari enthused as she reached them, hugging Faith first and her brother second. She beamed at both of them as she stepped back. "Oh, my. You two *are* a picture."

"Lucky I'm ready to take one, then," Nathan said, holding up his camera as Ryan shook hands with and greeted him, Marc and Father Mike. He introduced Faith to Marc and Father Mike.

"It's very nice to meet you. I've known Ryan and Mari since they were as tall as my knee," Father Mike said, taking Faith's hand. "As you can see, a lot has changed since then," the priest joked, tilting his thumb at Ryan. The top of Father Mike's head currently was even with one of Ryan's silver shoulder boards.

"Father Mike married us, too," Marc said, taking Faith's hand.

Faith smiled tremulously. She'd worried before about the idea of having a priest marry them versus a justice of the peace. She understood from Mari that they had been brought up as Maronite Christians by their parents, who were very orthodox in their practice, even if Mari and Ryan had not remained strict adherents as adults. Having a priest marry them seemed so much more...*binding* than a justice of the peace, although Ryan had assured her that when it came to the law, which is why they were marrying, it made no difference whatsoever.

She'd *previously* had those doubts.

As she stood there at Ryan's side with all those kind, smiling people, the spring day surrounding them like a blessing, she was glad they'd get married by an old family friend…a man of God.

"Well, should we proceed?" Father Mike asked, waving toward the blossoming groves, a twinkle in his eye.

"Absolutely," Ryan said, his eyes on Faith, his gaze warmer than the sunshine. He held out his arm for her, and she took it.

Later she wished she could remember more details of the brief ceremony. It was as if the whole experience passed in a blaze of sensation: golden sunshine, brilliant blooms, the sweet scent wafting off the trees, the sound of the waves breaking on the beach in the distance…the warm, steady look in Ryan's eyes as they repeated their vows. She recalled the cool sensation of the white gold on her skin as Ryan slipped the ring on her finger, the sound of Father Mike's voice saying, *I now pronounce you husband and wife.* She remembered the radiant expression on Mari's face as she looked on, tears spilling down her cheek.

But she'd never forget the first time Ryan kissed her as her husband.

His mouth felt warm and cherishing as it moved over hers. When they parted, a thrill of anticipation went through her when she saw the possessive gleam in his eyes.

Clarisse served them lunch on the terrace, where they sat in shade and looked out on to a sunny, sparkling Lake Michigan. Ryan hardly saw the view, however, as busy as he was touching Faith's bare shoulder and staring. She looked more radiant than he'd ever seen her.

He managed to tear his gaze off her for a split second and saw Marc looking at his wife, his head close to hers.

"Do you remember the last time we sat at this table? You were pregnant then, too," he murmured.

"Of course I remember," she said softly, exchanging a meaningful glance with her husband. "This place is charmed. That's why I suggested it for you two." She transferred her gaze to Ryan and Faith. Faith looked up at him shyly. He leaned down to kiss her mouth.

"So you two plan to just return home after this?" Mari asked later, after they'd eaten the delicious cake Clarisse had prepared for them from scratch.

Ryan cupped Faith's shoulder in the palm of his hand and squeezed lightly. Was that a blush spreading on her cheeks as she toyed with her cake fork?

"That's right," Ryan said. "I was wondering if I can have a word with you before we leave, Marc?"

Everyone at the table stilled, but Marc looked the most stunned of all at Ryan's request.

"Sure," Marc said. He took his napkin from his lap and pointed toward the picturesque stone path that ran between the lake bluff and the orchard. "Do you want to take a walk?"

Ryan nodded, gave Faith a smile and one last squeeze of her petal-soft shoulder, and stood. Mari looked puzzled and a little worried about Ryan's request to talk to Marc in private. He felt guilty about that and tried to give her a reassuring smile. His sister had put up with his unresolved issues with Marc Kavanaugh for too long, now.

He and Marc walked for a ways in silence, finally pausing when they reached a low, circular stone wall that served as a lookout to the lake. They stood gazing out at the rippling, sun-dappled water.

"I've been reading in the papers that the polls have you far ahead of your opponent for the senate race," Ryan began. "It looks like we're going to have a U.S. Senator in the family."

Marc made a doubtful noise. "Anything can change between now and November."

"It won't," Ryan said, sitting on the stone wall. "Remember when we were in high school, and I used to say you'd probably be president some day?"

Marc gave a wry smile. "And you were going to be my Air Force One pilot."

"I still will be, if the need should ever arise," Ryan said, grinning swiftly.

"It won't. I would never put Mari through that mess. This campaign has been hard enough on the family. I'll go back to being a prosecutor after I serve my term," Marc said.

Marc spoke amiably enough, but Ryan noticed his slightly puzzled expression. He couldn't understand why Ryan had called him out here for this little discussion.

"I have something that I want to…confess, I guess," Ryan said after a pause.

"Okay," Marc said slowly, his brows bunching together in consternation.

He exhaled and looked out at the dancing water. "When Mari first told me she was pregnant with Riley, when I took her back to San Francisco with me, there were a few times that I encouraged her not to tell you she was going to have your baby."

Only the waves crashing on the beach broke the stony silence that followed.

"She never agreed, of course. I know now that I was wrong to tell her that," Ryan said. "I'm sorry."

"And you realize that because of your experience with Faith?" Marc asked. "You wouldn't want to be cut out of the picture any more than I would have, would you?"

"No," Ryan said, meeting his onetime friend's stare. Anger sparked in Marc's blue eyes. "And in answer to your question about Faith, *yes*. That was part of why I wanted to bring up the topic to you today. But there's more."

"Go on," Marc said after a tense moment.

"The accident happened a long, long time ago. In a different lifetime. I won't lie that I've been angry and resentful about losing my parents. I took out a lot of my anger on you, but I know you didn't deserve it. It hasn't been fair, to you, or to Mari or to Riley." He looked at Marc. "We used to be friends once. Good friends."

"The best," Marc said grimly.

He watched a wave break on a rock, sending up a tall spray.

"You've made Mari so happy. More happy than she's ever been in her life. I've considered Riley as my family, but not you," Ryan stated baldly. He looked at Marc. "I want that to change. I want you to be a real uncle to my child, just like I am to Riley. I want us to be brothers. *If* you can see your way to forgive all my misplaced anger over the years, that is."

"Of course I forgive you. If you can forgive me in the same way," Marc said.

He stood and held out his hand. Marc shook it.

"What's family for, if not to forgive our worst faults?" Ryan asked with a small smile.

"Exactly," Marc agreed. He slapped Ryan's upper arm. "Now, let's get you back to your bride."

"Ryan? Why did you want to talk to Marc earlier? You guys looked so serious when you left. And when you got back, you both seemed...relieved."

Ryan opened the front door for her. The house felt a little stuffy, so Faith flipped the air-conditioning on low. She turned to face Ryan.

"I was saying something to him that I should have said a long time ago," Ryan said, removing his coat. "I guess you could say that the specialness of the day sort of...popped it out of me."

The specialness of the day.

His words reverberated in her brain. That, along with some other phrases that had kept reoccurring with alarming frequency as she'd sat by Ryan's side during the lunch, exquisitely aware of his touch on her shoulder and arm. Phrases like, *I, Faith, take you, Ryan, to be my wedded husband.*

Or Father Mike saying, *an institution ordained by God, which is not to be entered into lightly or unadvisedly.*

Faith took a step toward him.

"It was a special day, Ryan. I want to thank you. It...it couldn't have been any lovelier if we'd planned it for a year."

He draped his coat on the back of a chair

and stepped toward her, his eyes intense. "Did you really think so?"

"Yes," she whispered.

"You felt it, too?"

She swallowed. She knew precisely what he meant. No matter how much she wanted to cling on to the comfort of a marriage of convenience, something *larger* than she'd expected had happened out in the orchard today. Call it the divinely inspired weather, or the fact that Ryan was the most handsome, dashing man she'd ever laid eyes on, or her own foolish heart, but the day would forever be treasured in her memory.

"Yes," she said softly. "I felt it."

He stepped closer to her. She looked up at him solemnly. He touched her cheek.

"The day isn't over yet. Let's make it last, Faith."

She swallowed through a constricted throat. She knew exactly what he meant, of course. There was no other way to interpret the hot, possessive gleam in his eyes.

"I'm not sure that'd be a good idea. It's not what we planned."

He opened his hand along the side of her neck. His other hand caressed her shoulder, reminding her of how aware—how excited—she'd been while he stroked her during their wedding lunch. He lowered his head.

"To hell with the plan. Life isn't meant to be planned. It's meant to be..."

"Lived," she finished for him shakily. She looked into his eyes. He didn't move. She knew he wouldn't, either. He was waiting for her.

She placed her hand on the back of his head and pushed him down to her. She fit her mouth to his, sliding and caressing, nibbling at him...memorizing the feel of him. When she slicked the tip of her tongue between his closed lips, she felt his body leap in arousal next to hers. He groaned, his hands sliding to her waist.

His kiss was like chained desire set free. Faith gave herself to it—to him—completely. Doubt and fear were for another day, not this sunny, glorious, blessed one.

Not her wedding day.

Ryan took her hand and led her down the hallway. He hesitated in front of his bedroom.

"Should we...here?" he asked, waving at the door.

Faith nodded. Her mouth suddenly felt

too dry to speak. "Yes," she managed. "It's all new."

He gave her a small smile of understanding and started to lead her into the bedroom. He looked back when Faith didn't follow.

"I'm going to go and change," she said breathlessly. Heat scalded her cheeks. "I'll be right back."

He just nodded. It was so odd to consider Ryan off balance, so she couldn't be sure, but she had the strangest impression he was speechless.

She hurried to her bedroom and closed the door. She pulled an ivory-colored silk negligee from her drawer. The exquisite nightgown had been ordered from an online catalogue. Faith hadn't allowed herself to dwell for long on why she'd bought it. She told herself that it'd been an impulse buy. Didn't she deserve to spoil herself with luxurious, sexy things once in a while?

She certainly hadn't allowed herself to consider the meaning of the fact that she'd made the order the day after she'd called Ryan and agreed to marry him.

Changing quickly, she then brushed her hair until it shone. She could see her pulse throbbing at her throat when she inspected her reflection.

Moments later she tapped lightly at Ryan's partially opened door.

"Come in," he said.

He turned from where he'd been standing at his open closet, a leather belt in his hand. He froze when he saw her. Never taking his eyes off her, he draped the belt on a hook and spun to face her. He wore only the dark blue trousers from his uniform.

"You look beautiful," he said, his voice low.

"So do you," she said sincerely, giving him a shaky smile.

He came toward her. Suddenly she was in his arms, surrounded by his solid male strength and breathing in the subtle, spicy scent of his aftershave. That full, wonderful feeling she'd been experiencing on and off all day swelled tight in her chest cavity.

"Are you sure you want to do this, Faith?" he murmured, his gaze scoring her.

"Yes. Today, I'm sure," she whispered.

His nostrils flared slightly. He bent to kiss her and their mouths fused. Just like during their wedding, a brilliant palette of sensation suffused her consciousness. His mouth was so demanding, and yet so gentle, warm and firm. His smooth skin and dense muscles flowed like a sensual blessing through her seeking fingers. He parted her lips with his tongue, and she felt herself melting into him. She delved her fingertips into the thick, crisp hair on his head and pushed him down closer to her. He bent his knees and put his hands on her hips, pressing their bodies almost as close as a man and woman could get.

Almost.

She gave a soft cry when he lifted her and carried her over to the bed.

"I've waited for this for what feels like forever," he said after he'd laid her on the bed. He stood over her, his expression almost grim with desire as he looked down at her.

"Let's not wait anymore," she said, reaching for him.

He came down over her, pressing her into the mattress. She loved his solid weight, adored the way he kissed her with feverish possession. She felt burned by him, scorched by his intensity. She made a sound of protest when he broke their kiss and rolled onto his side, his front facing her. He placed his hand below her ribs. It looked dark and masculine next to the pale, soft fabric. Her breath stuck in her lungs when he ran his hand over the fullness of her breasts. He brushed the thin straps off her shoulders and lowered the fabric.

For a few seconds he said nothing as he stared at her bare breasts. His heated gaze caused an ache of longing at her core.

"So beautiful. So feminine." He touched the side of a breast. "So soft." His gaze rose to meet hers. She stilled when she saw the deep emotion in his dark eyes. "Our child is going to nurse here, one day."

"Yes," she mouthed.

"Faith…" he whispered heatedly. She watched, enthralled, as his dark head dipped. She trembled as she watched him kiss a pink nipple, then slip it between his lips. Her entire body seemed to sizzle in sympathy with the flesh in his warm mouth when he drew on her so sweetly.

A sharp cry broke free of her lips.

His large hand closed gently over her other breast, his fingertips gently manipulating the beading center. He shaped her to his palm and lifted his head, holding her breast in his hand and slipping the other nipple into his mouth.

She whimpered in rising need and raked her fingers through his thick hair. Desire pinched at her almost painfully, but he seemed so intent on his task, she couldn't bear to make him stop. She stared sightlessly at the ceiling while he teased and manipulated and worshipped her sensitive flesh, mounting her desire unbearably.

"Ryan," she finally pleaded softly.

He lifted his head from her flushed, aching breasts. His eyelids looked heavy with arousal.

"I'm sorry," he whispered, his hand moving along her sides, stroking her sensitive skin even as he lowered the fabric down over her waist, and then her hips. Soon, she was lying before him, naked. His gaze burned her. His hands followed, worshiping and stimulating all at once. He traced the shape of her hip and thigh with his palm, and then lowered his head to her stomach. She moaned at the sensation of his open mouth on her belly button, the ache at the center of her becoming unbearable. She clamped her thighs shut to alleviate the pressure.

"Shhhh," he soothed, rising over her, his hip next to hers, one elbow bracing him. He touched between her thighs, his fingertips gentle and knowing. He kissed her mouth softly when she cried out.

"Open your thighs, Faith," he whispered hoarsely next to her lips.

She hadn't realized she'd been closing them so tightly, as if she was unconsciously protecting herself from the rush of sensation and feeling that would come if she exposed herself. She looked at Ryan through heavy eyelids, his face so rigid with desire, and knew she'd been foolish to try to keep herself separate from him…safe from him.

Only a coward would keep themselves safe from the one they loved.

She parted her thighs. A slight convulsion went through his tight facial muscles.

"Oh, Faith," he muttered thickly. "You're so sweet."

"Ryan," she whispered, trembling. His hand moved, tenderly exploring the folds of her sex, granting pleasure wherever he touched.

He kissed her, and she tasted the salt of the sheen of sweat from his upper lip. Or was that from her tears? His fingers stroked her and the pleasurable friction mounted. Her hand moved frantically along his shoulders and neck, clutching spasmodically as the pressure swelled.

"All those flowers out there today, and here's the loveliest one by far," she heard him say as if from a great distance. She cried out sharply as pleasure broke over her. Ryan kissed her deliberately while she shook, making sure she could breathe, but seeming to relish the sensation of parted lips and her small cries falling past his own. His warm hand remained between her thighs, coaxing every last shudder of pleasure from her flesh.

Faith blinked a moment later, coming back to herself. Her eyes widened when she saw that Ryan had removed his pants. He lay next to her naked, his thigh draped over her leg. She felt his firm, warm arousal pressed against her hip.

She moved without conscious thought, touching him. He shut his eyes and made a low, restrained sound in his throat. He felt so heavy in her sliding palm, the skin softer to the touch than she would have expected...like warm silk stretched tight over steel.

"Faith," he mumbled, his voice gravely with arousal. She met his gaze and continued to caress him. "Will it…will it hurt the baby?"

"No," she whispered. "Absolutely not. The baby is very well protected, and I'm a low-risk pregnancy."

He stretched toward the bedside table. She watched, wide-eyed as he rolled on a condom, and then he was coming over her, his arms taking his upper-body weight, his hips between her opened thighs.

A cry of amazement leaked out of her lips when he entered her slowly. He paused.

Every muscle in his body looked like it was flexed tight and hard. It was a wondrous sight.

"I don't want to hurt you," he grated out.

She touched his narrow hips. "You're not hurting anything. It feels wonderful," she whispered. She urged him with her hands, welcoming him.

His groan sounded like it was ripped out of him. Faith cried out shakily, for suddenly she was filled with Ryan again, and he throbbed high and deep inside her. How could she have forgotten how exquisite the sensation was?

How right.

He began to move, and pleasure rippled through her in shocking waves. She watched his face, and knew he experienced the same bliss, that their desire fused them, made them one. He stroked her faster, and her entire world began to quake. Sweat gleamed on his rigid muscles as he took them both higher, and she joined in the dance, moving in the rhythm he set with perfect synchrony.

She gritted her teeth together and cried out in longing when she felt his desire swell hard and deeper inside her. He paused and bent his elbows, bringing his mouth to hers. As he kissed her again, both of them hovered on the edge of ecstasy.

"You're mine, Faith. Can't you feel it?"

She cried out sharply, his incendiary words igniting her release. She felt him move, sensed him straining, eager to leap into the fire with her.

Sharing that sweet, inevitable explosion of desire with Ryan hurled Faith into a whole new territory of existence.

Chapter Eleven

"Faith? Are you asleep?" Ryan asked her.

She smiled. She loved the sound of his deep voice roughed by both sleep and desire. They both lay on their side, Ryan spooning her. He moved his hand slowly and lazily across her bare belly, ribs and breasts. The sunlight filtering through the window had taken on the warm, golden cast of sunset.

"No," she said quietly.

"Do you love this house? I mean…was it your dream to always come back here as an adult?"

"No," she snorted. She glanced around

when he remained silent. Had he been super-serious? "I mean I *like* this house and every-thing, but I didn't buy it because of *that.* The circumstances just all collided. That's how I ended up here. I'd started my practice, and it was going really well. My parents were plan-ning to retire to Florida, and then Jesse died. So—" she shrugged "—I bought their house."

"Right," he said. "So it's not like it's your dream house or anything?"

"Hardly," she murmured.

"Is there space in the garage for me to set up a workshop? I want to get started on the baby's shelving unit."

She twisted her head farther on the pillow to see him better. He gently pushed her hair out of her face.

"My father had a workshop in the base-ment. Do you think that would work?"

His hand paused in the action of smoothing her hair. "Of course it would. I didn't know you had a basement."

"You didn't know *we* did," she corrected, smiling and snuggling back in the pillow.

His chuckle was low and gruff and de-licious. He swept his hand over her shoul-der and chest. "Is your father's workshop far enough away from the living area? I don't want to bother you with too much sound or a sawdust smell."

"There's good ventilation in it, and it's technically in a room beneath the garage. I should have thought to tell you about it before. I think it'd be perfect," she said, distracted because now he was caressing the upper swells of her breasts and it felt very good. She inhaled sharply when his fingertips detailed a nipple.

"Your breasts are extremely sensitive," he murmured, his mouth near her ear. She shivered at the sensation of his warm breath.

"From the pregnancy, I suppose."

She felt him harden next to her and hid a smile. They'd made love, and touched, and talked and repeated the cycle several times now, but Ryan didn't appear to be tiring of the routine.

"Not just from the pregnancy," he said. He slid his other arm beneath her and touched the other breast. Faith moaned softly, desire swelling in her yet again as he finessed both nipples at once. "I remember how sensitive they were on Christmas Eve." He shaped the flesh of one breast into his palm, molding and squeezing gently, while he continued to pluck at a nipple. She cried out shakily and instinctively curled her body into his, sealing their skin, feeling his arousal next to her backside. "How lovely they were," he continued to rasp in her ear. "If you had any idea how often I've thought about your breasts since then, you'd probably run for the hills."

She snorted with laughter, and then moaned as he took both of her breasts into his hands. "There aren't any hills around here."

He removed one hand and she heard the bedside drawer open.

"You'd run for a sand dune then," he assured gruffly a moment later.

He slid inside her at the same time his hand wedged between her thighs, stimulating her. Faith gasped in undiluted pleasure. He grunted gutturally as pulled her to him and flexed toward her at once, and their flesh fused.

He kissed her ear. "You're the sweetest thing in existence, bar none."

Morning sunlight peaked around the curtains as Ryan stuck his nose into the fragrant juncture of Faith's neck and shoulder. He nuzzled her. She stirred and murmured.

"Wake up," he said. "You may have plans to keep me in this bed as a slave to your every whim, but even slaves need food. Come on. Let's take a shower and I'll take you to brunch in town."

"I can make us something here," Faith mumbled sleepily.

"Uh-uh," he said, playfully slapping the sweet swell of her hip to rouse her. "You're not cooking. It's your honeymoon, remember?"

She looked over at him, her heavy eyelids widening slightly.

"Okay. It's not much of a honeymoon," he agreed. "But I'll make it up to you, someday."

Her smile made something curl tight in his gut. "It's been a wonderful honeymoon. I have no complaints whatsoever."

He rubbed her hip, considering. She looked downright edible, lying there with her dark hair in disarray on the pillow, the tops of her breasts peeking over the edge of the sheet, that sexy, thoroughly feminine smile shaping her lips.

"Okay, you talked me into it. Who needs

food," he growled, kissing her shoulder and neck hungrily. She broke into giggles and twisted away from him.

"No, no, you're right. We should eat. We never did last night."

He watched her getting up, disappointment swamping him when she picked up her nightgown from the floor and held it over her. Was he *nuts* for suggesting they get out of bed?

"Where are you going?" he asked, thoroughly bemused when Faith started to leave the room.

"To shower," she said, turning so that he could see the lovely profile of her back and rear end.

"The shower is right there," he said, scowling as he pointed to the bathroom adjoined to the bedroom.

"I have my own."

He rose from the bed like there was a fire. Her green eyes widened as he approached her.

"We'll shower together," he said, brushing her soft hair behind her shoulder.

He saw her nostrils flare slightly as she glanced down over him. He paused, his fingers in her hair, when he saw a flicker of uncertainty cross her features. He sighed and lowered his hand.

"I haven't seen that particular expression in over twenty-four hours now," he said quietly.

"What expression?" she asked.

"The doubtful one."

He saw her throat convulse as she swallowed.

"It's…it's not that, Ryan. I just need a little privacy, that's all. I'm… I'm not used to showering with anyone," she said awkwardly.

He sighed, hating to see her discomfort.

"I understand," he said. He kissed her quickly and urged her toward the door with a hand on her shoulder. "Hurry up getting ready, though. I want to show off my new wife."

She gave him a furtive glance over her shoulder and witnessed him admiring her backside. She threw him a repressive glance, hiding a smile.

He chuckled as she scurried out of the room, trying to ignore the disappointment he experienced at her going. Patience was what was required.

Winning Faith's trust would be a process, not a decisive battle.

* * *

They'd been blessed with a day that was every bit as glorious as their wedding day. They sat outside on the patio at Boatwerks on the edge of Lake Macatawa. Ryan attacked his Boatwerks biscuits with gusto. Faith watched him for a moment, grinning.

"You really are making me feel guilty now for keeping you in bed," she said.

He wiggled his eyebrows salaciously and forked up more fresh biscuit, sausage and poached egg. "A hard-working man has a big appetite."

Hard-*loving* man, she thought to herself. He grinned as if he'd read her thought and she laughed. She'd never seen him so playful, so carefree. It was a little addictive. Ryan was typically so hard, so...*strong*. She couldn't think of how else to describe him. He was rarely impassive with her, of course, but generally he exuded a steely, deliberate sort of male strength. He was the kind of man other men trusted immediately. If it weren't for the fact that he also possessed a potent sex appeal without even trying, Faith would have found him just as easy to trust.

She blinked when she recognized her

thought. Was she really going to hold it against him because he was so good-looking and appealing to the opposite sex? That seemed blatantly unfair—

"Are you going to eat?" Ryan asked, looking puzzled. Faith realized she'd paused with her fork hovering over her vegetable and cheese omelet.

"Oh, yes," she said, banishing her worries to the periphery of her consciousness.

After they'd eaten and paid the bill, they walked out onto the dock, breathing the fresh air off the lake and holding hands.

"I like that place," Ryan said, referring to Boatwerks. "Reminds me of the places I used to eat with my family when I was a kid."

They came to a stop at the end of the dock. "It must have been wonderful for you and Mari to spend the whole summer in Harbor Town."

"Yeah. Those summers went on for an eternity," Ryan murmured, looking lost in memory as he stared out at the lake. He gave her a sideways glance. "Or it seemed like they would at the time."

"That's one of the many wonderful things about children," Faith said. "A moment can stretch into eternity. I remember thinking that, growing up here in Holland," she said, nodding toward the lake, which was really a swollen, drowned river that stretched like a finger inland from the massive great lake.

Ryan nodded thoughtfully. "You were right. This part of Michigan really is ideal for raising a child." He squeezed her hand and she looked up at him. His short bangs flickered on his forehead in the soft breeze. He hadn't shaved this morning; his jaw was sexily shadowed by a scruff. His gaze on her was warm as he turned toward her, their middles brushing together.

"Thanks for bringing it back for me, how special it is here. After the accident all my great memories must have...receded into the background. They're still there. They didn't really disappear," he said, his gaze on the horizon as if he was seeing something Faith couldn't. He suddenly lowered his head to hers. A devilish smile tilted his lips. "When summer gets here, I'm going to take you to all my favorite beaches."

"No you won't," she scolded, grinning. "I'll be starting to show soon. There's no way in hell I'm putting on a swimsuit."

"You have a beautiful body," he said, pulling her closer in his arms. "Pregnant or not, you're gorgeous."

She narrowed her eyes on him in mock suspicion. "I read about men like you."

"What am I like?" he wondered, his gaze narrowed in a predatory fashion on her lips.

"The type that gets turned on by pregnant women."

His male laughter echoed across the bay. She chuckled, liking the sound. He bent, nuzzling her curving lips with his nose. "I don't get turned on by pregnant *women*." Their lips brushed together and his smile faded. "I get turned on by *you*, pregnant or not."

He proved the truth of his words with a deep, devouring kiss. He pressed with his hand at the small of her back and she arched into him. He leaned down over her, slaking his thirst. The warm sun shone down and the lake rippled around them, but Faith only knew the taste, scent and sensation of Ryan.

This is what it was to fall in love. *Really* fall in love, Faith thought dizzily when Ryan sealed their kiss. For an instant as she'd been under the spell of his kiss, the moment had stretched into an eternity.

But you're not a child anymore, an annoying voice cracked in her head. *You're an adult who should know that the magic always ends. Always.*

Ryan's hand tightened on hers. Her heart throbbed when he smiled. She silently told the offending voice to shut up, but it was very persistent.

"You have to be back at work tomorrow, don't you?" Ryan asked when they passed her office on the ride home.

She nodded regretfully. "I originally took today off with the intent of picking out paint for the nursery and choosing new carpet to have installed, and I haven't accomplished a thing yet."

He took her hand. "It was worth it, wasn't it?"

"Of course it was."

"I'll give you a real honeymoon sometime soon. You name the place and I'll fly you there."

A sharp pain went through her at his words. "That's not necessary, Ryan."

"Why not?"

She gave him a beseeching glance and

spoke before she could stop herself. "Because it wasn't a *real* wedding."

She immediately regretted it when she saw his jaw stiffen.

"I'm sorry," she said, wincing. What was wrong with her? She let go of his hand and stifled a curse. She didn't know why she'd felt the need to say it. Did it have something to do with the fact that she'd recognized fully just how vulnerable she'd made herself as she'd stood out on that dock with Ryan?

"Why should you be?" he asked, the hard sound of his voice making her wince again. "I know that's how you feel. It isn't like you haven't made it clear."

"You were the one who proposed the whole thing as a marriage of convenience for the baby, Ryan," she exclaimed.

He glanced at her, quick and sharp. She exhaled in disbelief. She felt burned by his stare.

"I know I said that then," he said as he drove, staring straight ahead. "But I meant what I said yesterday."

An hour later Faith was in the process of letting Topsy through the back door when Ryan walked into the kitchen. She glanced at him nervously. They hadn't really spoken since that uncomfortable conversation in the car. She'd been beating herself up repeatedly while he'd been down in the basement, apparently exploring the workshop area.

Despite her concern he seemed fairly relaxed as he paused by the counter holding the notebook in his hand that she recognized as being the one where he'd started sketches for the nursery bookshelves.

"I'm going out to the airport, and then to run some errands. I have to go to the sawmill to give some measurements for pieces for the shelving unit. I'm leaving for an overnight in San Francisco early tomorrow morning, so I want to get started on it while I can."

"Oh, okay," Faith said, feeling off balance by his friendly, relaxed manner, not to mention the news that he was leaving town again tomorrow. He'd told her that he was looking for another pilot now that he had two planes, along with an administrative assistant to help him with arranging flights and keeping the books. Until those employees were hired, however, she knew he and Scott would be extremely busy.

But despite all of that didn't he want to talk about what had happened in the car? Despite her outburst she wasn't at all sure she wanted to go back to respecting each other's space. She'd admitted to herself she'd fallen in love with Ryan, after all. Another part of her was sure she'd made a mistake yesterday by giving in to her desire for him, for falling prey to the magic of the day.

Her ambivalence seemed to be having the effect of freezing her up completely.

As far as Ryan went there could be little doubt he was swayed by the fact that they were going to have a child. She understood at this point, both from Mari and from Ryan himself, just how crucial family was to him. Their physical attraction for each other combined with his euphoria over becoming a father was confusing him into thinking he should spend the rest of his life with her.

"Are you okay?"

Faith blinked at the sound of his voice.

"Yes. Of course."

His dark eyes toured her face quickly before he spoke. "I'll probably stop by the hardware store on the way home for some supplies. Do you want me to pick up some paint and carpet samples for you?"

"That'd be terrific," she said gratefully.

He nodded once and turned to leave.

"Ryan."

"Yeah?" he asked calmly, looking over his shoulder.

She hesitated. She wanted to apologize for her outburst in the car, but she wasn't entirely certain she'd been wrong in what she'd said. Bewilderment swelled in her chest. She grabbed desperately for a certainty.

"I… I wanted to let you know that I have an appointment at the obstetrician's this Thursday. I don't think very much exciting is going to happen, but…well, you can come. If you have time. And…want to," she added lamely.

"Thursday at what time?"

"Two o'clock?"

"I'll make sure Scott is available on Thursday then," he said.

Faith stood there, watching helplessly as he walked away.

Ryan was gone for most of the day on Monday. When he finally did return home that night, he carried some wood and supplies with him. He greeted her pleasantly enough, explaining that the lumberyard would deliver the majority of the supplies for the bookcase later in the week. What he carried was just enough to get things started in a small way. He immediately disappeared into the basement, leaving Faith to stew in her confusion.

The next morning when she woke up in her room, Faith knew he was gone by the flat, empty feel to the house. She dragged herself out of bed with a heavy heart. Her work helped to ground her for the next two days. On Tuesday night, however, she succumbed to a wave of gloom, recalling the golden glory of the wedding in the tranquil, color-soaked orchard, the look in Ryan's eyes when he'd repeated his vows, the full, incendiary moment when he'd uttered those words...

You're mine, Faith. Can't you feel it?

Then she remembered all too clearly what she'd said in the car in a fit of fear.

Because it wasn't a real *wedding.*

A pain went through her at the memory, causing her to clutch at her chest. She walked out onto the back terrace and took deep breaths of the mild spring air, staring at the thousands of stars in the sky, and feeling her loneliness like an ache deep in her spirit.

The next afternoon at closing time, she was talking to Jane about a lab order and glanced up to see Brigit Kavanaugh walking into her office.

"Brigit! How wonderful to see you," Faith exclaimed. She came around the reception desk into the waiting area and greeted her friend with a hug.

"I haven't had a chance to offer my congratulations on your wedding," Brigit said, smiling. She handed Faith a flat, thin package wrapped in silver paper. "This is for you."

"Oh, thank you! You shouldn't have, Brigit."

"It's not much. Derry and I had one from an aunt of mine, and I always treasured it."

Faith gave her a warm smile. "Come back to my office and we'll chat."

"Go ahead and open it," Brigit encouraged a moment later after they'd both sat in chairs in her sunny office. "Ryan won't mind. He's a man, and this is something that goes in the china cabinet. I'm quite sure Derry never had a clue what was in ours."

Faith laughed and unwrapped the gift. Inside the box was a lovely sterling silver filigreed platter with a simple inscription bearing their names and the date of their wedding. Seeing Brigit's thoughtful gift made tears well in her eyes for some reason. Much to her embarrassment, they spilled down her cheeks unchecked.

"Oh, I'm sorry. It's…just beautiful," Faith managed shakily as she hastily dried her cheeks with the back of her hand.

Brigit reached for some tissues on her desk and passed them to her, looking mildly concerned. "Is everything all right, Faith?"

"Oh, yes," Faith assured. She glanced into Brigit's face, however, and another shudder of emotion went through her. More tears spilled down her cheeks. She'd never had a nurturing, overly involved mother figure in her life, and something about Brigit's kind, concerned expression at that moment undid her. She sobbed, holding the tissue to her face as if to hide from her misery when she felt Brigit's touch on her shoulder. "It's just…well… I'm pregnant, Brigit," she wailed, as if that explained everything.

Which, perhaps, it did.

Brigit just made soothing sounds while she had her cry. After a minute she took several more tissues and mopped up her face, feeling contrite.

"I'm really sorry," she mumbled. "I feel

like I cry at the drop of a hat these days. The platter is absolutely beautiful."

Brigit waved her elegant hand, making it clear her gift was hardly crucial.

"How far along are you?" Brigit asked.

"Fifteen weeks," Faith hiccupped.

"And Ryan..."

"Is the father, yes. He came to my house last Christmas Eve—after he spent the holiday with you and your family, actually," Faith explained wetly. "He said he wanted to see if I was all right. He and Jesse were...good friends, you know," she said brokenly. She inhaled to calm herself, but more tears spilled down her cheeks. "That's when it happened. The baby I mean. Well...everything."

She swallowed painfully and gave Brigit an apologetic glance, saw that the older woman's face was tight with understanding. She stroked Faith's shoulder as another wave of emotion shuddered through her.

"And so you two decided to marry because of the baby?" Brigit asked.

Faith nodded, ignoring the new tears that spilled down her cheeks this time. They just seemed to keep coming.

"It's supposed to be in name only," she said

miserably. Brigit patted her when her face clenched up and she sobbed again quietly.

"Shhhh, try to calm down now, honey," Brigit murmured comfortingly. She stood and made her way to a small refrigerator Faith kept in her office. She opened the bottle of water she found there and handed it to Faith. Faith thankfully took several sips of the cool water, feeling herself calm.

"From what you've said so far, I'm gathering that you care about Ryan," Brigit said, sitting down across from her again.

Faith just nodded.

"And how does he feel about you?"

"He thinks he cares about me, but it's all wrapped up in his need to sort of…protect me or something ever since Jesse died. We're attracted to each other. Obviously," Faith said, glancing down at her stomach and then back up at Brigit. When she saw a look of amusement pass over Brigit's face, she couldn't help but grin tiredly. "Oh, Brigit," she said, shaking her head. "How is anybody supposed to know *what* they feel in a strange situation like this one?"

"Are you talking about you, or Ryan?"

"Both, I suppose. Ryan is being incredibly

sweet about the baby. He's very excited. Mari told me he's always wanted to have a child."

Brigit nodded. "I can see that. The Itanis were a very close-knit family, and Ryan has always been loyal to the bone. I had reason to resent his familial loyalty after the accident and during the lawsuit, but that was years and years ago. I understand his need now to protect Mari—his only family—and provide her with whatever compensation was available to her for the loss of their parents. Not that money can replace a loved one, but... well..." She faded off for a moment, looking thoughtful. "Ryan was practically a kid himself then, but he took on the full responsibility of a man, making all the decisions and fulfilling all the obligations that came along with the death of both of his parents."

Faith sniffed. "I guess I'm not the only one he gets protective over."

Brigit smiled and patted her hand. "He cares deeply about his sister. For a while she was his only living family. If Ryan is concerned for you, it means he cares."

Faith's lower lip trembled. She wanted to believe what Brigit said was true, but...

"But he's gone so much, Brigit. He's a pilot...like Jesse."

Brigit's blue eyes sharpened on her. "Oh, I see."

Faith blushed. Brigit Kavanaugh could be quite formidable, at times. When Brigit said she saw, she *saw* with that incising gaze of hers.

"You're afraid that Ryan is going to turn out to be the rootless, womanizing type."

Faith said nothing, but her cheeks turned warmer.

Brigit sighed after a moment. "There are no guarantees when it comes to marriage, Faith. But if it helps you any to hear it, I've known Ryan since he was about six years old. He and Marc were best friends. In the summer months he was practically one of my own children, he was around the house so much. By the time he was thirteen, practically every girl in Harbor Town had a crush on him, including my Deidre," she added wryly.

Faith smiled uneasily.

"Lots of men as good-looking, as athletic and smart as a boy like Ryan would have let it go to their head. But he wasn't like that. He had girlfriends, all right, but to my knowledge, he was always loyal to them. And trust me, I would have heard about it if he wasn't, with two teenage daughters in the house who somehow always knew what everyone else in Harbor Town was doing."

Faith laughed.

"There. That's better," Brigit said, her gaze warm on Faith.

"Thank you, Brigit," she said, squeezing the other woman's hand.

"It's my pleasure. I wish I could say something more to assure you. In the end I think the only thing you can do, though, is take it one day at a time. Try to trust in Ryan unless you see some clear reason you shouldn't. I know it's hard, when you've known heartache and betrayal. Trust me. I *know.* Derry and I made our mistakes in the early part of our marriage, and there were times I wondered if I'd ever be able to trust him again. But in the end, you either choose to have faith or not. I know it's like tying a blindfold around your eyes and walking along a ledge. It's terrifying, but it gets easier over time. And that's just…"

"Life," Faith whispered, giving Brigit a grateful smile. She stared out the window on to the sunny day, feeling the shadows of her doubts recede into the corners of her mind.

Chapter Twelve

Faith left her bedroom hastily that night when she heard the front door open at around seven. Ryan paused at the entryway of the living room when he saw her.

"Hi," she said, smiling.

"Hi."

For a second or two they just stood there, gazing at each other. He looked wonderful to her, wearing a pair of dark jeans and a blue-and-white button-down shirt, his overnight bag slung over his shoulder. The mail had come late today. He clutched the envelopes in one hand. As usual his good looks and utterly masculine aura left her a little breath-less. Would it feel like this every time he returned home after an absence?

"Did you have a good trip?"

"Yeah," he said, taking a step into the room. "I met with Nick Malone while I was out there. He told me that I can take Eagle Air as far as I want. DuBois Enterprises can give me enough work to keep nine or ten planes moving alone, and that doesn't even include the new business contacts I've made. I'm thinking of keeping some hangar space in the Bay Area, as well, and keeping some planes there for a more convenient turnaround."

She beamed at him. "Ryan, that's wonder-ful. Nick really believes in your work ethic."

He shrugged and swung his overnight bag off his shoulder. "He's ex-Air Force, too," he said, as if that explained all Nick's faith in him.

"I think it's more than just that," Faith said, smiling knowingly. She noticed him turn his head toward the kitchen and wondered if he'd caught the aroma of the chicken she had bak-ing. "Are you hungry?"

"I'm starving."

"Good. I made baked chicken and home-made potato salad."

"Sounds great," he said, but she saw puzzlement flicker across his features. Obviously he was confused about her running from hot to cold to hot. She inhaled slowly for courage and stepped toward him.

"Ryan, I want to apologize for what I said in the car the other day. It was wrong of me. I shouldn't have been so disrespectful about the good feelings we were having, being together. I was…scared."

She saw his throat convulse as he looked at her. "I know. I understand."

She sighed and gave a small laugh. "I'm glad one of us does, then. My point is, I realized while you were gone that we just have to take this one day at a time. I'll try not to give in to my insecurities, but that's all I can really promise for now."

"One day at a time is good enough for me."

She gave him a tremulous smile. "Thank you, Ryan." She straightened and took a deep breath. "Now…dinner is almost ready. Do you want to take a shower before we eat?"

"If there's time."

"There's time," she told him with a smile before she walked to the kitchen.

Faith set the table in the dining room, complete with lit candelabra. "Wow, I've never eaten in here before," Ryan said when he entered, looking appealing in jeans and a fresh shirt, his dark hair still slightly wet.

"Too bad it's not a very fancy meal," Faith said, setting their filled plates on the table.

"Fancy or not, it's fantastic," Ryan said a few minutes later as he ate, appearing to completely appreciate her efforts.

They talked comfortably enough during dinner about some immediate plans for Eagle Air, including the fact that Ryan was interviewing two potential candidates for the administrative assistant position in addition to a pilot the following morning.

"I'll still be available for the doctor's appointment, though," he said after they'd finished eating, but they remained sitting at the table, sipping their water and iced tea. "Have you been feeling all right?"

"Yes. Very good, actually. I haven't been tired at all at the office for the past few days."

"Good. I'm glad," he said, reaching up to touch her hand where it rested on her placemat. It seemed like a completely natural gesture, given their comfort with one another during dinner. But as he continued to stroke her hand warmly, and prickles of pleasurable sensation shot through her arm, Faith became aware of a shift in the atmosphere. She glanced at him hesitantly and saw that his eyes were on her, dark and intense.

"Earlier you said one day at a time," he said quietly. "And I'll do whatever I can to make this work for you, Faith. But I have to be honest—now that I've made love to you again, I'm not sure I can go back to abstinence. It just doesn't seem…natural to be here in this house with you and not touch you."

Her cheeks warmed. She looked at her plate. "I understand. For some things, it's impossible to go backward. I hadn't really expected that we could, either."

He squeezed her hand softly. She met his stare.

"And you're okay with that?"

"Yes. I don't want to run anymore from what's happening between us," she said in a hushed tone.

He nodded slowly, still stroking her wrist with his thumb.

"I appreciate you saying that. I know this isn't easy for you."

"Making love with you is the easiest, nicest thing in the world, Ryan. It's not that part that's hard."

His expression went flat. His caressing thumb stilled. She sensed his incredulity at her words.

"You honestly didn't think I wasn't loving *that* part, did you, Ryan?"

He blinked, as if awakening from a trance. "To be honest, I wasn't quite sure what to think after Monday morning."

"I know. I'm sorry."

"I didn't mean for you to apologize again."

"I know," she whispered.

He inhaled slowly. "Why don't you go and relax while I clean up the dishes?"

"That's not necessary, I can—"

He surprised her by leaning across the corner of the table and kissing her, quick and potent.

"You cooked. I'll clean up."

"Okay," she said when she'd recovered her voice. "Maybe I'll just go...take a shower." Despite what she'd said, she remained seated, and so did he. Faith grasped for her courage and finally found it. "You can sleep in my room tonight. If you want."

He raised his eyebrows in a subtle, wry gesture that said loud and clear that he most certainly *wanted*. Faith chuckled softly, and he smiled.

Faith was in bed when he tapped on the door later. She wore a dark green nightgown that left her shoulders and a good portion of her chest bare. Her skin gleamed in the golden light of the lamp. Her dark hair was piled on her head, but some of the rebellious tendrils had escaped down her back and coiled at her shoulders. She was wearing glasses and reading a publication called the *American Journal of Veterinary Research.* He paused next to the door, his body going on instant alert at the tempting sight she made.

He closed the door and approached the bed, smiling.

"Looks like fascinating reading," he said.

"Oh, it is," she said so confidently that his smile widened. She had to be the most adorable woman he'd ever seen. Her green eyes flickered down over his bare torso, making his nerves tickle in awareness, and landed on the envelope he carried.

"What's that?" she asked.

He sat on the edge of the bed. She scooted over, giving him room. He hesitated for a second. Maybe this wasn't such a good idea. She might think he had mercenary reasons for his actions, but in truth, he'd done what he'd done out of concern for Faith and their child.

He handed her the envelope. She opened it, a curious expression on her face, and withdrew the papers inside.

"I had these medical tests done just before the wedding. I know with the baby, you've probably had lots of blood tests done to make sure you were healthy. I thought it was only fair for me to do the same. I wasn't promiscuous when I was single, by any stretch of the imagination, but I wasn't abstinent, either. I've always practiced safe sex, Faith," he said in a quieter tone.

She glanced up at him, a startled expression on her face.

"Except for Christmas Eve," he said sheepishly. "I thought maybe given our first night together, you might have very good reason to doubt my assurances in that regard." He nodded toward the envelope. "I got a completely clean bill of health."

"Ryan, you didn't have to do this," she said, her voice shaking a little.

"Yes, I did," he said firmly. He took the papers and set them on the bedside table. The journal she'd been reading slid off her blanket-covered thighs onto the floor, but neither of them paid any notice. He took her hand.

"I'm not going to be with another woman, Faith. Not for as long as we're together."

Tears swelled in her eyes. "I'm not going to be with anyone else, either," she said in a choked voice.

He leaned forward and caught her soft gasp with his mouth. Her arms flew around his neck, and she pulled him closer. He came down on the bed, partially sprawled on her, kissing her like she was his very breath. Her scent filled his nose—flowers and some singular scent that came from her skin. He came up for air from their kiss and buried his nose in the fragrant juncture of her neck and shoulder.

"I can't believe I was only gone for two days. It feels like weeks since I touched you," he said between feverish kisses. A shudder went through him at the sensation of finger-nails scraping his scalp.

"I missed you, too," she said breathlessly.

His mouth coasted down her throat, nib-bling hungrily at her skin. She moaned and grabbed at his waist when he gently took a love bite from her shoulder. He'd never known a flame of desire to leap so high and powerful so quickly as it did with Faith. It was like he existed constantly on a low simmer for her, and a touch, a kiss, could send that fire to the boiling point instantly.

He ran his mouth over her chest, breath-ing her scent, testing her skin with his lips and tongue. Her hands moved restlessly over the bare skin of his back, making him shiver un-controllably. He felt need swell in him, hard and hot, as he moved his lips over the lace of her nightgown and the upper swells of her breasts. He tugged on the straps of her gown, suddenly impatient to taste her…drown in her sweetness.

She cried out sharply when he slipped a nipple between his lips and drew on her, so he softened, laving his tongue over the stiff-ening tip, soothing and exciting her at once. His hunger mounted soon enough, however, breaking through his feeble restraints when it came to Faith. He gently gathered her breast in his hand, molding her softly to his palm, while he applied a steady suction with his mouth. She tasted like woman and sex and something so sweet, so precious, he couldn't find the word if he tried.

He pushed her gown down lower. The skin over her ribs tasted just as good, and so did the exquisitely soft stretch along her sensitive sides. He heard her whimpers of excitement through the sound of his heart pounding in his ears as he licked and kissed and nibbled at the skin there. An almost unbearable ache of longing went through him when he kissed her abdomen. Was it his imagination, or had it swelled slightly even since the last time he'd kissed her there? It felt so warm, taut and smooth beneath his cherishing lips.

Her fingernails raking his scalp—this time more forcefully—added a welcome spice to his excitement as he kissed the tender strip of skin below the slight swell of her belly and ran his hands along her silky thighs. He lifted his head and worked her gown down over her legs. He sensed the tension rise in her muscles when he lowered her panties. For a few strained seconds he just looked down at her, stunned by her beauty. He glanced up at her face and saw the glaze of desire in her eyes.

A ripple of excitement went through her when he kissed her just above her pelvis. He lowered his head, closed his eyes and tasted her for the first time. He moaned softly, and was lost.

He was gentle with her, focusing exclusively on the soft, nectar-sweet folds of her outer sex and the precious kernel of nerve-packed flesh nestled between them. The essence of Faith filled him, her flavor, her scent, the sexy sounds of her soft whimpers and increasingly desperate moans.

She called his name wildly when she bucked in release. He came at her bidding, waiting until she'd quieted beneath his kiss.

When he slid into her, his mouth fused to hers, it was like a sharp blade of distilled pleasure knifing through his flesh. He'd only ever been inside a woman naked once before. Faith had been his first.

As he began to move, and ecstasy became his entire world, Ryan sent up a silent prayer that she would be his last.

Ryan and Faith stood when Dr. Feingold, her obstetrician, greeted them both in the waiting area of the clinic.

"Are you the baby's father?" the friendly doctor, who was in her late forties, asked Ryan unabashedly.

"Yes."

"Would you like him to come back for your visit?" Dr. Feingold asked Faith.

"Yes, that'd be wonderful," Faith said, giving Ryan a warm smile. He seemed a little embarrassed, walking back with her and Dr. Feingold to the exam room, but all in all, she thought he handled the appointment with calm aplomb. It was a singularly female environment, of course, decorated in soft colors with tasteful paintings on the wall, many of them alluding to the theme of mother and child, or families. They passed several women in varying stages of pregnancy in the hallway.

After Dr. Feingold had completed her brief exam, she asked Ryan if he had any questions for her. Much to Faith's surprise, he did. He asked first about how frequently Faith would need to come for prenatal care from now until the pregnancy was over. Then he asked about the pros and cons of ultrasounds.

"We'll do an ultrasound for the fetal anatomy survey in…" Dr. Feingold flipped through Faith's chart. "Four weeks, just to make sure all is well with the fetus. Faith is very healthy. She's a low-risk pregnancy. If all goes well, there won't be any need for another ultrasound after that."

"Will we be able to identify the sex then, if we choose to?" Ryan asked.

"Absolutely," Dr. Feingold said.

"One last question. Should Faith be painting the nursery? I can do the regular painting, but she's been planning to do a wall mural."

Faith blinked in surprise. Why hadn't she thought to ask about that?

"We generally recommend that someone else do the painting, Faith," Dr. Feingold said kindly. "It's probably too low of a toxicity to matter, but might as well play it safe, right? Luckily enough, you seem to have an interested party here," she said, smiling at Ryan, "or you can just wait to do the project after the baby is born."

Faith glanced at Ryan a little shyly on the way home from the appointment.

"What?" he asked, noticing her covert stare.

"Nothing. It's just…have you been reading up on pregnancy and prenatal care? I just thought…because of those questions you asked during the appointment…"

"Sure I have," he said matter-of-factly. He stopped at a stoplight. "It's my first baby, too, Faith."

"I'm so glad you asked that question about the paint. Thank you."

She grinned. She couldn't help it. It was so…nice to think of him caring enough to research the pregnancy on his own, amazing to think of him looking out for her. He smiled along with her, and suddenly all her concerns about the wisdom of her relationship with Ryan were millions of miles away.

Ryan was crazy busy for the next two weeks. He hired an administrative assistant and got her set up in the small office space he was renting at the airport. He also hired a new pilot, an ex-Navy, ex-commercial airline pilot who was in her fifties and looking for full-time work now that her two children were off at college. The new hire, whose name was Sylvia Aaron, gave Ryan a tip about a medium-turbo prop plane for sale in Detroit. Ryan was interested in adding a larger plane to his fleet, something that could fly up to ten passengers at a time to conferences or larger meetings. He did an overnight trip to Detroit, and came home the following day triumphant at his latest purchase.

"Congratulations!" Faith enthused when he'd given her his good news. She gave him a huge hug and a kiss, the latter of which ended up lasting for the better part of several minutes. When they finally broke apart, she smiled as he rained hungry kisses on her cheek and neck.

"I missed you," he said.

"I missed you, too," she replied, distracted by the movements of his mouth on her throat. "But, Ryan…before you get carried away—"

He gave her a slightly harassed look when she pried herself out of his arms. She grinned at his surly expression. He reminded her a little of how Topsy might look if she gave her a dish filled with food, only to whip it away at the last second.

"I have a surprise for you. I had a feeling you were going to get the plane. I made you a special dinner."

She beamed a moment later when she saw his expression of pleasant surprise when she showed him what she'd made him.

"*Shish taouk,*" she said excitedly, referring to the white meat chicken skewers that she'd grilled. The dish smelled delicious, the meat having been marinated in olive oil, lemon, parsley and sumac. She'd arranged it on the platter just as Mari had described, on a bed of saffron rice with a tahini sauce. "I got the recipe from Mari. She told me it was your favorite when you were a boy. I know it won't be anywhere near as good as your mother's or Mari's, but—"

"It'll be fantastic," he interrupted. He took the platter from her hands, set it on the counter and proceeded to kiss her even more fervently than he had upon his return home. When they finally broke apart, he said, "It's an awesome surprise. Thank you."

"You're welcome," she said, flushed with happiness.

He nipped quickly at her lips before he released her. "And guess what? I have a surprise for you, too. I'll show it to you tomorrow, after work. I'm a little worried you won't like it, but...well, we'll see I guess."

No matter how much she prodded him, he wouldn't give her a hint as to the nature of his surprise. After dinner, they made love. Faith was drifting contentedly into sleep, surrounded by Ryan's arms, when his cell phone started to ring on the bedside table.

She sat up drowsily when he moved, turning over on her side to face him. It was a little late for someone to be calling. Through heavy eyelids, she watched him answer.

"Hello?"

His brow furrowed as he listened.

"Oh...hi," he said after a moment. He gave Faith a flickering glance and sat up straighter in bed. She sensed his tension. Her nerves prickled into alertness when she distantly heard a female's voice resounding from the receiver. Whoever it was, she sounded upset.

"I don't know. I don't think that'd be a very good idea," Ryan said cautiously. This time, Faith was sure of it. His glance at her was furtive. Wary.

It suddenly felt as if lead had replaced her insides when he suddenly stood and walked out of the room, closing the door behind him, the phone still pressed to his ear.

Faith just lay there, trying to sort out why the phone call had upset her so much. She realized it was because she'd been in this position before. She'd been with Jesse a few times—maybe more times than she cared to remember—when he'd gotten a phone call and suddenly walked out of the room. It wasn't until that moment, that very moment, that Faith realized those awkward phone calls had probably been from other women.

His lovers.

The realization had just never hit her until now. She'd found out about Jesse's infidelities while he'd still been overseas. He'd died soon afterward. She'd never had any reason to put two and two together and resolve puzzling little moments like that from her previous marriage.

Feeling cold and heavy, Faith turned over and curled up beneath the covers. When Ryan came back to bed later, she pretended to be sleeping.

By the next afternoon her glacial insides had thawed out quite a bit. Her busy day at her office had gone a long way to bringing her around to her senses. That phone call last night might have been anything—an old school friend, an old girlfriend, even his new female employee, for all she knew. By the time Ryan walked through her office front door to pick her up, she'd recalled what Brigit had told her.

Try to trust in Ryan unless you see some clear reason why you shouldn't.

He certainly had done nothing offensive, she reminded herself. She became so disgusted with her paranoia that she vowed to herself not to even ask him about the strange phone call.

When he came to her office to pick her up at around five-thirty that evening, he seemed preoccupied.

"Are you all right?" she asked him when they got in the car and he pulled out of the parking lot. "You seem sort of...worried or something."

"No, no I'm fine. Well, maybe a little concerned. But it'll be okay," he seemed to say to himself as much as to her. "If you don't like it, it's no big deal. You're not under any obligation to—"

"Ryan, what in the world are you talking about?" she interrupted, starting to get worried now herself.

"You'll see," he said, giving her a smile of reassurance and grabbing her hand.

"Are we going to visit Brigit?" she asked a

while later when he drove into Harbor Town and turned right onto Sycamore Avenue. "Is Mari in town or something?"

"No. It's not that."

"Well, what th…" She paused when he slowed down the car, staring out the window in bewilderment when he pulled into the drive of the house she recognized as being the large, handsome one that had once been the Itani summer home. A woman wearing a beige-colored suit walked down the front steps as if to greet them. Faith gaped, aghast, when she saw that the for sale sign that had conspicuously been displayed when they'd passed weeks ago was missing.

"Ryan," she began numbly. "You didn't… we're not…"

"I put down a small fee to hold this house until you saw it," he said quietly. "I'd like to buy it, Faith. For us."

Chapter Thirteen

"What? *Why?*" Faith asked, utterly floored.

He took her hand. "It's a beautiful house. I don't know when it'll come up for sale again, if ever." Ryan scanned her expression, looking anxious.

Faith's dazed shock was fractured slightly when she saw movement near Ryan's window. He glanced around.

"That's Mrs. Reynolds, the real estate agent. Why don't you just take a look at the house? You don't have to say yes. It's not like I put down a full down payment or anything,

I just asked her to put it on hold for us until the weekend."

Faith managed to shake her head and mutter a passable greeting to a smiling Mrs. Reynolds. Her numbness fractured slightly when she entered the beautiful home and saw the gleaming hardwood floors, the spacious rooms, the luxurious kitchen, the wonderful detailing and craftsmanship that had gone into the building of the house. She'd regained the power of speech by the time they entered the dining room with the lovely built-in china cabinet and elegant chandelier.

"This was your family's *summer* home?" she asked Ryan in weak disbelief. She knew that Ryan's father was a top executive for a car company in Detroit, but she'd never really thought before about how affluent Ryan's life must have been growing up.

"Yeah, but I don't remember ever eating in this dining room once. We always ate on the back terrace or in the kitchen during the summertime," he said, smiling in memory. She pictured it, Mari and Ryan—both of them suntanned and full of the buoyancy of youth—sitting on the shaded back terrace with the lovely climbing hydrangea in full bloom, regaling their parents with stories of their day's adventures. Suddenly the image altered and she saw Ryan and she sitting at the same patio table, listening patiently to their dark-haired child's excited retelling of their day.

They were touring one of the large, well-proportioned bedroom suites, which was filled with golden evening sunlight when Ryan suddenly asked Mrs. Reynolds if they could have some privacy. The real estate agent gave them a knowing glance, assured them she'd be out on the front porch, and told them to take their time.

"I hope I didn't upset you," Ryan said quietly, studying her from across the large room.

"You didn't upset me! But I can't figure out what you were thinking," she exclaimed, a large measure of her incredulity sweeping over her again now that they were alone.

"You don't like the house?" he asked.

"Are you kidding? It's amazing. It's perfect. I've never even considered living in a house like this. I grew up in this area. I know what a house like this so close to the beach must cost."

"I can afford it."

She stared at him, mute.

"Mari and I both received large trusts from our parents' estate. I spent my entire adult life in the service. The military provided me with almost everything I needed. I didn't have to spend as much as most people, so I was able to save a lot of money. Invest."

Her mouth had gone dry. "But, Ryan, that's your money."

"It's ours," he said firmly, stepping toward her. His face looked gilded and solemn in the luminescent, golden light. "We're married, Faith."

Unexpectedly the topic of their future had come up again. She hadn't prepared for it. She didn't know what to say.

Ryan touched her shoulder. She looked up at him helplessly.

"I know when I first brought up the topic of marriage, I said we could divorce after the baby is born. I'll still do whatever you want in that regard, Faith. But you must know by now that isn't what *I* want. I'd like us to remain as a family." He touched her cheek. "I'd like that more than anything. But no matter what you decide about the house, I'm still considering buying it as an investment property."

He glanced around the sunny room. "It hurt to give up this house before. I'd like to keep it in the family."

Utterly caught in his solemn-eyed stare, she jumped slightly when his cell phone began to ring. He muttered under his breath and reached into his pocket to get it. He scowled when he saw the number, tapped a button and stuffed the phone back in his pocket.

"Aren't you going to answer it?" Faith asked bemusedly.

"No," he said. He reached for her hand. "Did I happen to mention this was my bedroom, growing up?"

"It was?" Faith asked, glancing around for a fresh take on the room.

"Yeah. Come on. Let me show you the master bedroom. I have some ideas for renovation in there that'd make it incredible…"

"What are you thinking?" Ryan asked her later on the drive back to Holland.

Faith bit at her bottom lip anxiously. The idea of moving into that gorgeous home with Ryan, of raising their child there, was like being told an amazing dream could come true. But in order for them to step so firmly into the future, didn't they need to confirm their feelings for one another? Was it really enough for Ryan to choose a future based solely on his love for family and his child?

Wasn't love and partnership important, as well?

She realized that Ryan was patiently awaiting her answer.

"I think it was incredibly generous of you to make this offer, Ryan. The house is fantastic. And you're right...a house like that doesn't go up on the market frequently in Harbor Town. I can understand why you'd want to own it again. They tend to be kept in families for generations."

"I'm glad you liked it."

"I loved it," she said, looking at him as he drove. "Do you think I could have a little time to think over the idea of us moving there together, though?"

"Of course."

"Thank you," Faith said, her heart filled with the strangest, most potent combination of dread and hope at once.

The next afternoon she retired to her office after her last patient and sank into her office chair. She was surprised she'd gotten any work done, she'd been so preoccupied with making the decision about the house. Of course the house was only at the surface of the core of the dilemma. Ryan hadn't probably meant to do it, but by showing her that home last night, he'd brought the entire issue of their arranged marriage to a head.

In order to make such a game-altering decision, she knew she had no choice but to put all her cards on the table and hope that Ryan did the same.

She was going to have to bite the bullet and tell Ryan that she'd fallen in love with him. How else was it possible for him to make an informed choice about his future? How else was it conceivable for her? She was going to have to march home and tell him the truth.

When she saw his reaction to the fact that she loved him, body and soul, she'd have her answer as to how to proceed.

Ryan was down in the workshop assembling one of the many units of the bookshelf when he heard knocking at the front door. Had Faith forgotten her key? He glanced around hastily for his shirt, but didn't see where he'd tossed it when he'd whipped it off earlier. The air-conditioning didn't work very well here in the basement, and he'd been working up a sweat.

"Coming," he shouted as he lunged up the stairs, two at a time. "Did you forget your—"

He paused in midsentence as he flung open the front door when he saw Jesse's old girl-friend, Melanie Shane, standing on the front stoop.

"I told you I didn't think it was a good idea for you to come here," Ryan said coolly a minute after he'd let Melanie inside. They stood in the living room, exchanging tense words.

A tear leaked down Melanie's face. She'd always been a good-looking woman, but her appearance had altered since Ryan had last seen her while they were both still stationed in Afghanistan. After Jesse had died, she'd started to lose weight. She'd lost even more since Ryan had left the service. Weight loss agreed with Melanie, making her voluptuous curves more streamlined and her blue eyes larger and even more haunted in appearance than they'd been when Ryan had last seen her.

"I had to come," she said, her usually

cigarette-roughed, tough-girl voice trembling with emotion. "You're the only person I could talk to, Ryan. You were Jesse's good friend. The only one who knew how close Jesse and I were. I mean... I know you didn't entirely approve of Jesse's and my relationship, but you're the only one who could understand what his death meant to me. I've left the Air Force," she said starkly after a pause.

"You did?"

She nodded and sniffed. Ryan sighed and walked across the room to get her some tissues.

"Look, Melanie, I've got nothing against you, but—"

"Don't give me that line, Ryan." Her jaw tilted up defiantly. "I know you always looked down on my and Jesse's relationship. I suppose you thought even less of me because of that night we celebrated Shaunessy's birthday."

Ryan didn't reply. He just stuck out the box of Kleenex tissues for Melanie. If she wanted to rehash the night she'd gotten drunk at Mike Shaunessy's party and come on to Ryan because Jesse had been flirting heavily with a nurse from the hospital, she was going to have to do it with someone else. It wasn't as if he hated Melanie. He actually felt sorry for her, and he had a good idea of why she was here...

...why she was feeling so miserable in regard to Jesse's death.

But there was nothing he could do for her. He couldn't offer Melanie the peace—or the solace—for which she longed.

"Like I've been telling you when you've called the past couple times, there's nothing for us to discuss, Melanie. I want you to go. This is Faith's home. You know that. You shouldn't be here. It's disrespectful."

Melanie's eyes flashed with anger at that. Her gaze landed on a photo on the corner table of Faith holding a tiny version of Topsy up to her cheek.

"So that's the paragon of virtue herself," Melanie said scathingly. She glanced around the house as if seeing it for the first time. Her gaze landed on Ryan. She gave him a thoroughly amused feminine appraisal, her eyes lowering over his naked torso. "I can't believe you married Jesse's widow. Isn't that a little...*sick*?"

"Get out," Ryan said quietly.

He'd been hoping to get rid of Melanie politely, but that clearly wasn't going to happen. Melanie could be all right at times, but she also could get herself worked up into a real state. Jesse had used to joke that he didn't know whether to dread or adore Melanie's temper tantrums, because they were hell to endure, but heaven to make up from.

"So you really envied Jesse his sappy, sweet little animal-loving wife. Funny," Melanie said, stepping closer to him, her voice going husky, "I would have pegged you above all men for needing a strong, hot-blooded female."

Ryan halted her attempt to press against him by grabbing her elbows.

"Cut it out, Melanie. What are you trying to prove by acting so stupid?" he asked, his patience running thin. "It's not going to get you anywhere here with me. No more than it ever did," he seethed.

As if his angry words had popped a cap off a geyser, she sobbed, her entire body heaving with uncontrollable emotion.

"Oh, God, Ryan, I know you know the truth. I know you know the real reason I'm here. I can't stand it anymore. You're the only one who knew how badly Jesse and I had been fighting before we got that emergency call about Langley's plane going down in the Kunar. You're the only one who knows the truth. *I* killed Jesse and the others."

Ryan ground his teeth together as she shook with misery. Here it was. Melanie had been piloting the chopper that had gone down on the rescue mission. He exhaled, wishing like hell Melanie had chosen another time and another place to have her little mental breakdown.

Still…she was a soldier in arms and more importantly, another pilot. What she was experiencing right now was every pilot's worst nightmare. He couldn't help but feel compassion for her.

"You didn't kill Jesse or anyone. It was an accident, pure and simple. You were down low, on the lookout for Langley, and the chopper hit a power line. You know as well as I do other choppers have run into similar problems with those low lines. They're a menace."

"But if Jesse and I hadn't been arguing before, maybe I would have been less distracted and more alert. Maybe—"

"It wasn't your fault," Ryan repeated, tightening his hold on her upper arms. She was near hysteria. Her guilt must have been build-ing up in her for a while now. "I know a pilot feels total responsibility for their passengers and mission, but that's not the same as say-ing that you killed someone. It was an *acci-dent*. Those wires are uncharted and damn near invisible outside of twenty feet. There was nothing you could have done," he said, shaking her slightly, trying to break through her misery.

"I loved him," Melanie said in a strained, vibrating voice. "I know you don't believe I'm capable of it, but I am. I miss him so much." She collapsed against him. Ryan gripped her tighter, trying to keep her from falling.

"Melanie," Ryan pleaded.

"I have never, ever loved like this. It hurts so much," she said against his chest, her hands grasping at his shoulders desperately.

Ryan opened his mouth, wildly searching for something to say that would bring both comfort and closure to this awkward situation. He glanced over Melanie's head and froze.

Faith stood at the entryway to the living room, holding a sack of groceries, her green eyes huge, wearing an expression he'd seen before on shell-shocked soldiers.

* * *

Faith was so stunned she didn't at first know how to interpret what she was seeing. Ryan held a tall, willowy blonde against him. The image of the woman's red-tipped fingernails clutching at the dense muscle of his naked shoulders was scored on her consciousness, as was Ryan's returned tight hold on her upper arms.

"I have never, ever loved like this. It hurts so much," she heard the woman moan as if through a barrier of thick cotton. Her fingers clutched tighter at Ryan.

"Faith."

She looked up into his face. It looked rigid with tension. The woman whipped her head around. Her face was wet with tears.

"I…this is Melanie," Ryan said in gruff tone. "Melanie Shane."

"Hello," Faith said hollowly. She hardly knew what she was saying. She hardly knew what she was doing as she set down the grocery bag on a nearby table. A strange noise had started up in her ears, like a fierce wind blowing.

"Excuse me."

"Faith," Ryan's voice came from just behind her a few seconds later as she walked toward her car. "That wasn't…it wasn't what it might have looked like. Let me explain."

"So that's Melanie?" Faith asked as she opened her car door. Ryan caught it. They stood in the driveway, separated by the door.

"Yes. She shouldn't have come here. I'm sorry. I've been telling her not to, but she's upset. She wanted to talk to me about—"

"You weren't being entirely honest when you said *some* men would find her attractive. She's very pretty. You shouldn't leave her standing in there alone, Ryan," she said flatly before she got in the car.

"Dammit, Faith—" He lifted his hands to try and reach for her and she swung the door closed. Hard. He whipped his hands out of the opening just before the door would have banged forcefully into his fingers. Faith started up the car and put it into Reverse. He thumped his hand on the window as it began to move away from him. "Faith, come back here. You're jumping to the wrong conclusion," he boomed.

But Faith could hardly hear him. Her heart was beating like she'd just narrowly escaped the monster trap of a lifetime.

She blinked fifteen minutes later when she saw the sign welcoming her to Harbor Town's city limits. She'd driven blindly, unaware of any goal or destination.

Or had her numb brain perhaps chosen this route purposefully, to remind her of all she'd been about to put on the line…all she'd been about to sacrifice by exposing her soul and taking a chance on the future with Ryan?

She pulled into the parking lot of White Sands Beach. She'd chosen the location randomly, seeing its entrance from Travertine Road. It had suddenly struck her that she should pull over. She felt ill. She shouldn't be driving. It wasn't safe.

She just sat there behind the wheel of the car for the better part of an hour, staring at the sparkling lake in the distance, waiting for her brain to stop vibrating in shock.

What the hell had just happened?

She closed her eyes and tried to piece together the events of the past several hours. Her brain didn't seem to be working properly, and she felt as if she might throw up.

She'd decided to pick up the ingredients for a nice dinner for Ryan. She wanted to lay everything on the line…tell him the truth.

She was in love with him. If he didn't balk at her admission, if he, too, thought they had a future together as a true husband and wife, she'd be able to read it in his face. She knew somehow that she'd see his hesitancy once she admitted she loved him.

If there was one thing she knew about Ryan, it was that he worried about her. He'd feel responsible if he asked her to continue the marriage for the sake of the baby and him having the family he'd always wanted, knowing all along that he risked hurting her because she'd truly fallen for him.

She'd made that risky choice, and returned home with her heart on her sleeve, so to speak. And then...

The image of the woman's red fingernails clutching at Ryan's naked shoulders flashed into her mind's eye like a visual slap to the face. Suddenly she knew for a fact that had been Melanie who had been calling Ryan for the past several days. A pain went through her and faded to a dull, cramp-like ache. She clutched at her abdomen, applying a slight pressure, trying to soothe it.

So *that* had been Melanie Shane. Jesse's lover.

She'd certainly seemed close to Ryan, as well.

Ryan had insisted she'd misunderstood what she'd seen, but what she'd seen had been pretty damn inflammatory.

Since Melanie had contacted her by email, breaking the news about her affair with Jesse, Faith had imagined the other woman countless times. She knew it'd been stupid, but she defied any wife who discovered that her husband had been cheating not to wonder about the other woman.

Imagining Jesse with Melanie Shane had been nothing...absolutely *nothing* to seeing Ryan holding her.

The vision of the lake blurred before her eyes. Faith opened the car door and vomited. Another cramp went through her. She bent over in the car seat, gasping for air.

For the first time real fear pierced her chaotic emotional state.

Chapter Fourteen

Ryan plowed through the doors leading to the Acute Care Unit at Harbor Town Memorial, barely moving in time to stop from plowing into a maid's cart and knocking over all her supplies.

"Sorry," he said, not pausing to stop in his rapid forward motion. "Is the Acute Care Unit down that way?" he asked the startled maid, pointing toward the hallway to the left. The woman nodded, her eyes wide.

Ryan plunged down the hallway, ignoring the nurses' station.

"Sir. Can I help you?" one of the nurses called after him, standing. "Sir, you're going to have to come back here!"

"It's all right," Ryan heard a woman say. "Ryan!"

He paused, panting. He didn't want to stop until he located Faith, but whoever this was knew his name. Maybe she knew which room was Faith's—

God, let her be all right, he thought as he whipped around.

"Dr. Feingold," he said, recognizing Faith's obstetrician as she came toward him. "What happened? Where is she? Is she okay?"

"Yes," Dr. Feingold said firmly, staring straight at him as she approached, as if she wanted to make sure she had his complete attention. "She's absolutely fine. And so is the baby."

Ryan exhaled raggedly. He'd been in a panic ever since he'd received the phone call from an intake nurse at the Emergency Room at Harbor Town Hospital.

I'm afraid your wife came into the E.R. earlier. She'd been experiencing some pretty severe cramping and spotting. We've contacted Dr. Feingold, your wife's obstetrician. She's on staff here at Harbor Town Memorial. The doctor has arrived and has ordered a series of tests. She'd like to admit Faith. That's all we know right now, sir, the nurse had added when Ryan had demanded to know if Faith would be all right.

He'd driven to Harbor Town in record time, the entire time his brain ablaze with wild concern and regrets. What if something terrible happened to Faith and he'd never told her he loved her? If there was one thing he'd thought he'd had on his side, it was time. Surely Faith would learn to trust him, the more time they spent together. Surely she'd gain faith that the only thing he wanted to do was to see her happy...to know she was loved.

Her shattered expression as she'd stood there looking at Melanie Shane in his arms earlier rose up to haunt him. That was the reason she'd grown ill. He hadn't intended to hurt her in any way, but he had, nevertheless.

"I want to see her," Ryan demanded. "Where is she, Dr. Feingold?"

"She's resting. She's in Room 212. But why don't you sit down over here for a second with me. You look very shaken up. I'll explain about the test results."

Renewed terror tore through him. "You said she'd be all right."

"And she *will* be," Dr. Feingold assured,

urging him to sit down next to her on a bench. Ryan sat stiffly.

"What happened?" Ryan asked.

"She was having some breakthrough bleeding and some cramping. She was right to come into the Emergency Room. We did all the routine tests, though, and everything is fine, both with Faith and the fetus."

"Why was she bleeding then?"

"It's not uncommon. Lots of women have spotting while they're pregnant. It was more the cramping I was concerned about, but as it turns out, Faith had vomited. Her cramps were more associated with an upset stomach than the baby."

Ryan nodded numbly. "She was upset," he mumbled, his gaze turning down the hallway. "I have to see her, Dr. Feingold."

"All right. Just try to keep her calm. I'm going to keep her overnight, just for observation. She can go home in the morning."

Ryan nodded, barely hearing the doctor, his entire focus on seeing Faith.

Faith stared out the hospital room window. Light was fading. It would soon be night. It was funny, how a scare like the one she'd just been through made you reconsider so much, really made you appreciate the things you daily overlooked and took for granted, like the beauty of a new day or the simple touch or smile of a loved one. A visit to the hospital really made you think about what was important, and what wasn't.

She turned eagerly at the sound of the knock at her door.

"Ryan," she called, smiling. Tears burned in her eyelids. He looked so tall and straight and wonderful...and *worried*, she realized regretfully as he entered the room.

"I'm so glad to see you," she said, a rush of love going through her at the sight of him. "The baby is going to be okay. Did anyone tell you?"

She couldn't quite read his expression as he came next to the bed.

"Ryan? Did you hear me?" she asked. "The baby is going to be fine."

His dark eyes looked desperate...a little wild.

"I only wanted to know you were all right," he said.

For a few seconds they just stared at each other. What he'd said had pierced straight to her heart. Why had she been so certain he was only interested in her out of pity because of Jesse's infidelities or because she carried his child? How else could she possibly interpret the worry and love pouring out of his eyes at this very minute?

"Oh, Ryan, I'm so sorry about running off like that without letting you explain. It's just…Jesse…and Melanie…and seeing you holding her," she choked out tearfully.

"She's been trying to get in contact with me because she's carrying around a guilt complex about the crash. She feels responsible."

Faith froze. "Was she?"

"No. It's not uncommon for a pilot to feel that way after an accident. I'm not best friends with Melanie or anything, but I do feel bad for her. It's hard for a pilot not to feel compassion for another one in that situation. It's all of our worst nightmare. Anyway, Melanie misses Jesse and was breaking down when you walked in. I've been telling her it was inappropriate for her to come to your house, but she's been so persistent—"

"I figured it was probably something like that, once I had the chance to really think about it. Being in the hospital like this, feeling terrified that something was wrong with the baby…well, it really gives you a chance to reflect on things," she said, sobbing softly.

"Don't get upset, honey. Please," Ryan implored.

"No, no, it's okay. I'm all right. I'm just sorry for judging you like that."

"It's okay," he said, his heart plastered all over his usually impassive, top-gun facade. He set his hip on the bed and hugged her tightly.

"Oh, Ryan, I love you," she said in a pressured fashion against his shirt.

"I love you, too, Faith," he said, running his hand over her hair, soothing her. "I think I've been in love with you since Christmas Eve. At first I doubted what I was feeling. Later, after I returned to Michigan, I started to trust in it. But I could tell you weren't going to buy it after all you'd been through with Jesse… with me…with us falling for each other so hard and so fast."

She sniffed and rubbed her cheek against his shirt. "I should have trusted you, Ryan. I should have trusted this," she said, hugging him closer to her.

He cupped her head in his hand, urging her

to lean her head back. She did so, never finding the sight of his face so compelling as she did at that moment, with his love exposed.

"I told myself all we needed was time," he said. "I knew I could gain your trust...your love if I just had the time to prove myself to you. After today I realized that I might never have any of those things."

"No," she whispered fervently, hating the haunted look that shadowed his rugged features. She pressed her lips to his warmly. "You have all those things—time, trust and love. My love, most of all."

Epilogue

Ethan Kassim Itani's first day at the new house on Sycamore Avenue was the family's first day, as well. It felt like living a miracle to Faith to walk into their beautiful new home carrying her beautiful new son.

"I'll take him, so you can look around better," Ryan said quietly when they reached the landing at the top of the stairs of the house.

"Oh, *Ryan*," Faith whispered as she looked at the newly polished floors and painted walls. The house on Sycamore Avenue had been beautiful when they'd viewed it four and a half months ago, but what Ryan had done to it in the meantime made it downright stunning.

"I can't believe it, you painted the hallway and put in the wall sconces," she breathed, glancing around in wonder. "You've been working too hard, doing this and everything with the business, too," she admonished as she turned to hand him the bundle in her arms. She looked down into Ethan's tiny face as Ryan took him. The baby wrinkled his nose and made a pursing movement with his mouth before he resumed sleeping again. Faith glanced up into Ryan's face and they shared a smile.

"The most gorgeous baby in the world, the most beautiful house and the most wonderful husband," Faith whispered. "How is it possible for one woman to feel so much happiness at once?"

"Does that mean you can't take any more?"

She grinned and narrowed her gaze on him. "What do you mean?" she asked suspiciously. "Did you finish the nursery?"

His grin widened. He led her down the hallway. She gasped when she walked into the room. Faith had insisted on putting up the stenciling for the wall mural, even though she wouldn't be able to actually paint it until after the baby was born, so that part remained unfinished. Ryan had completed every other possible conceivable detail of the nursery, however. The walls were painted in a rich cobalt-blue, the white furniture they'd chosen contrasting with it handsomely. She walked over to the finished, dark walnut shelving unit that Ryan had fashioned, admiring the gleaming wood and all the useful cabinets and shelves.

Tears smarted in her eyes when she turned to face her husband and son.

"It's perfect. It's absolutely perfect," she said.

"Come here," he said, his gaze on her warm. She hugged him around his waist, careful not to wake Ethan. She smiled at her beautiful boys.

"Should we see how Ethan likes his new cradle?" she asked. Ryan nodded and she watched, spellbound, as he laid the baby inside and gently covered him.

He turned and took Faith into his arms.

"To think," she whispered. "You used to sleep in this room at night and dream about the next day's summertime adventure."

A smile tilted Ryan's mouth. Warmth and love suffused every pore of her being when

Ryan leaned down and fastened his mouth to hers.

"And one day," he said quietly next to her upturned lips a moment later, "Ethan will scheme up his own dreams, and a whole new generation of adventures will take place in Harbor Town."

* * * * *

HOMETOWN HEARTS ♥

YES! Please send me **The Hometown Hearts Collection** in Larger Print. This collection begins with 3 FREE books and 2 FREE gifts in the first shipment. Along with my 3 free books, I'll also get the next 4 books from the Hometown Hearts Collection, in LARGER PRINT, which I may either return and owe nothing, or keep for the low price of $4.99 U.S./ $5.89 CDN each plus $2.99 for shipping and handling per shipment*. If I decide to continue, about once a month for 8 months I will get 6 or 7 more books, but will only need to pay for 4. That means 2 or 3 books in every shipment will be FREE! If I decide to keep the entire collection, I'll have paid for only 32 books because 19 books are FREE! I understand that accepting the 3 free books and gifts places me under no obligation to buy anything. I can always return a shipment and cancel at any time. My free books and gifts are mine to keep no matter what I decide.

262 HCN 3432 462 HCN 3432

Name	(PLEASE PRINT)	
Address		Apt. #
City	State/Prov.	Zip/Postal Code

Signature (if under 18, a parent or guardian must sign)

Mail to the **Reader Service:**

IN U.S.A.: P.O. Box 1867, Buffalo, NY. 14240-1867
IN CANADA: P.O. Box 609, Fort Erie, Ontario L2A 5X3

* Terms and prices subject to change without notice. Prices do not include applicable taxes. Sales tax applicable in NY. Canadian residents will be charged applicable taxes. This offer is limited to one order per household. All orders subject to approval. Credit or debit balances in a customer's account(s) may be offset by any other outstanding balance owed by or to the customer. Please allow 4 to 6 weeks for delivery. Offer available while quantities last. Offer not available to Quebec residents.

Get 2 Free Books,

Plus 2 Free Gifts—

just for trying the Reader Service!

Get 2 Free Books,

Plus 2 Free Gifts— just for trying the Reader Service!

Get 2 Free Books,
Plus 2 Free Gifts—
just for trying the Reader Service!

Get 2 Free Books,
Plus 2 Free Gifts—
just for trying the Reader Service!

HWI7R

READERSERVICE.COM

Manage your account online!

- Review your order history
- Manage your payments
- Update your address

*We've designed the
Reader Service website
just for you.*

Enjoy all the features!

- Discover new series available to you,
  and read excerpts from any series.
- Respond to mailings and special
  monthly offers.
- Browse the Bonus Bucks catalog and
  online-only exculsives.
- Share your feedback.

Visit us at:
ReaderService.com